The Man
on the Train

The Rhys Davies
Short Story Award Anthology

Cynan Jones is from near Aberaeron, on the west coast of Wales. His acclaimed fiction, which includes five novels and numerous short stories, has appeared in over 20 countries, and in journals and magazines including *Granta, Freeman's* and the *New Yorker*. He also writes for screen, has written a collection of tales for children, and a number of stories for BBC Radio, including the twelve-story collection *Stillicide*. He has been longlisted and shortlisted for numerous awards, and won, among other prizes, the Wales Book of the Year Fiction Prize, a Jerwood Fiction Uncovered Award, and the BBC National Short Story Award. His short story collection, *Pulse*, is forthcoming from Granta Books in November 2025. Website: www.cynanjones.net

Originally from Belfast, **Elaine Canning** is a literary prize and festival director, writer, and editor. She holds an MA and PhD in Hispanic Studies from Queen's University, Belfast and an MA in Creative Writing from Swansea University. She is currently Head of Strategic Public and Cultural Engagement at Swansea University, including Director of the International Dylan Thomas Prize, the Rhys Davies National Short Story Award, and the Cultural Institute. Elaine has authored a monograph and papers on Spanish Golden-Age drama, and her short stories have appeared in *Nation.Cymru* and *The Lonely Crowd*. Editor of various short story and poetry anthologies, including *Dictionary of Light: The Rhys Davies Short Story Award Anthology* (Parthian, 2024) and *New World, New Beginnings: Resilience and Connectivity through Poetry* (Parthian, 2021), she is also editor of *Maggie O'Farrell: Contemporary Critical Perspectives* (Bloomsbury, 2024). Her debut novel, The *Sandstone City*, was published in 2022 and featured on *Wales Arts Review*'s 2022 list of top ten long-form fiction titles.

Elaine is a Fellow of the Learned Society of Wales, a British Council Wales Board member, a literacy champion for the National Literacy Trust, and a member of the reading promotion sub-committee of the Books Council of Wales. www.elainecanning.co.uk

The Man
on the Train

The Rhys Davies
Short Story Award Anthology

Edited by Elaine Canning
Selected and Introduced
by Cynan Jones

Parthian, Cardigan SA43 1ED
www.parthianbooks.com
ISBN 978-1-917140-89-8
First published in 2025 © the contributors
Editor: Elaine Canning
Selected and Introduced by Cynan Jones
Cover design by Syncopated Pandemonium
Typeset by Elaine Sharples www.typesetter.org.uk
Printed by 4edge Limited
Published with the financial support of the Books Council of Wales
Printed on FSC accredited paper

Contents

Introduction

Cynan Jones

Writing is not, in itself, fundamentally, a competitive act. At least, not in the sense that the act of writing competes with other acts of writing. But it is an act of striving. Or should be. The 'competition', then, is between the writer's ambition and the story they are trying to achieve; a competition which in the large part relies on a writer's technical ability, diligence, and their will to go as many rounds as needed to land the piece. It is a private competition, perhaps. And yet here we are again. Another writing prize. Another set of writers chosen over others. Or, rather, another set of stories, because – and by definition during a prize like this one, in which the writers behind the stories remain anonymous throughout the judging process – it is the *stories* themselves that have been chosen over others.

Judging a story competition is a difficult thing. A story can't outrun, out punch, out jump other stories it vies with. It can't up its game, shout louder, be funnier, change tactics. It turns up in a line, and that's that. That's all it's got. Then it's about the reader. And in the case of a competition, about the judge. The judge can't, or shouldn't, fall for the *potential* in a piece, that hasn't quite been achieved. The judge can't make edits or offer input to help fix a glitch. The judge can't suggest that a story starts later, or ends sooner, or that it would be better 'if'. Once it's entered into a prize, a story can't do anything about itself.

How, then, should a judge approach this difficult thing? Particularly in an award like this one, where there is only one judge. Where there is no recourse to conversation, no differences of opinion that can help change minds or draw the eye to things about a story that one person on their own might have missed, or mis-seen. Ultimately, the solo judge must set themselves some rules, abide by them, then test them, question those rules themselves! That's where the dialogue lies. Throughout this dialogue, though, some elements remained constants.

Technical ability on the page was a baseline for me. A good number of the stories that came through the filter process were not good enough on a technical level. That is, on a sentence-by-sentence level. That is not to say the writing was 'bad' in all cases. It is to say that the writer had not yet found the right register, or nuance to tell the story; or hadn't yet done enough rewriting of the story to quite hit the mark. There was potential in many of these stories, but this is a competition. There is no quarter.

Ambition was also key. Not simply the ambition to be ambitious. More a clarity of ambition. Stories with an idea of what they needed to be and to do, that set their stall out and didn't waver from that. Stories, ultimately, that asked the reader to trust them, then repaid that trust. These stories included not only stories that took narrative risks, that did brave things with text, but also stories that aimed at a too-easy-to-dismiss and very difficult to achieve subtler pace and understatement. Again, there were stories with ambition amongst those that didn't make the list. But that ambition hadn't quite been realised in the draft that turned up.

It also felt important not to hold one story up against another where both stories took on a similar theme. To resist the trap of making mini-competitions within the larger competition. The stories had to be judged in thematic isolation, against the rest of the pile. If two stories about surrogate children, for example, were both better achieved than the stories they were up against, then both deserved to go through. If then a third story about a surrogate child earned its place, so be it.

On the note of themes, it was marked how many stories had some commonality. In the very broadest terms, the vast majority of the entries spoke to one of three main themes, these being care, illness, or identity. This begs a question. Or, rather, it begged questions as I read through the pile. Were the filter judges drawn to stories with particular themes at their centre? Or are these the overriding themes of our time about which writers, writing currently, are moved to write?

As I read on, the stories themselves helped convince me the latter theory is true. Regardless of the success of the story on the page, there was tangible concern across the texts. There was a sense in pretty much all the stories of emotional urgency, however restrained, of a *need* to say something. There was an anger, I guess. Anger as a motivational force, enough to bring a person to the desk to find a story to be angry through. Sometimes this anger was overt; but often this anger was deeply bedded, felt part of a harrowed resting state somewhere far below the writer's surface.

I have judged, at this point, a lot of writing awards now. What has often stood out in past prizes is the underlying hope within the 'pile'. A hum of hope, poignant, subversive or blatant. That was there, this time, in *some* of the stories. But many ended leaving a sort of bafflement as to where we go next. It felt like many were written into a world in which it is less easy to believe that things will be all right.

Here we are then. The longlist. Despite the elaborations

above, I was given a straightforward task: there's the pile, pick the best twelve. It goes without saying the task gets harder as the process gets narrower. Then there's having to choose an ultimate winner. But I reiterate. A story will never know what it is up against, so it must be up against itself. The strongest possible version of itself. It must show an ambition to *do more* with the text, do more with the idea, to push beyond a 'reported' story and stay in the mind of the reader. To be something engaging, inhabited and memorable. I hope you find this selection all of those things.

The Man on the Train

Keza O'Neill

The man on the train is dying. Last night, he took an overdose of paracetamol. The generic kind, not the posh branded ones. Forty round chalky tablets. One for every year. He wanted to be sure.

Somewhere on the outskirts of Coventry, the train pauses at a red signal. A forlorn pony, stumpy legged with a matted coat, tears at the last vestiges of grass in a field that belongs to neither town nor country.

He didn't hurry. He prepared dinner to the soundtrack of retro *Top of the Pops*. Blur's 'Parklife' bounced across the silent walls. He basted rainbow trout in butter. A meal usually reserved for a special occasion. A film to follow, with the divine Dame Emma. He opened a good bottle of Merlot. Yes, yes, white wine with fish, but he's always preferred red. He took the pills in sets of three, rolling the rich, berry unctuousness of the wine around his mouth after each dose. It tasted of warmer places. Candy floss and cherries on a summer breeze. And something else? Those fizzy drinks you used to get in the '90s. The ones that were always slightly flat. What were they called?

'Any more tickets from Coventry?'

'Change at New Street for connections to Snow Hill.'

A cramp pricks his upper abdomen. He rolls his sweater and stuffs it under his neck.

Curl up. Try to sleep. Breathe.

He did his research. He knows what to expect. There is nothing peaceful about the method he has chosen, but other methods… the mess. The discovery. And what if he couldn't go through with it? So, hepatotoxicity then. A slow degradation. Cramping and nausea expected within the first twenty-four hours, followed perhaps by two or three days symptom-free. Then jaundice, blood clotting problems, confusion. Liver failure. Of course, it varies by individual. Genetics, existing liver damage, malnutrition, all come into play.

'Aberystwyth? Straight through to the end.'

Aberystwyth. Home. Can you call a place you haven't seen for twenty years *home*?

Nevertheless, it is where he is heading. This morning, the morning after the paracetamol, an unexpected tug. A compulsion to see the place again.

For after all, he knows what to expect. Five hours, two carriages, eighteen stations to Aberystwyth. The end of the line. A slow death of another kind. Which will come first: death or Aberystwyth? There's a joke in there somewhere. The man on the train has always used humour at inappropriate moments.

'Are you all right, love?'

He presses his eyes closed and attempts to breathe through the pain.

Those ridiculous sleep podcasts. MindFULLness. Less is what he craves.

Pay attention. Concentrate on your breath. Experience your environment with every sense.

Quiet your mind. If only.

Chant a mantra to still your thoughts, chirruped the smug American woman. *Keep it simple.*

He'd tried the days of the week. Was that a mantra? It was no good. He couldn't stop the uncompromising abyss of each day. Him, the air, his skin, his thoughts. Captive with himself in the relentless hours of nothing.

Monday was bin day. Three thickset lads heaved his black sacks onto a truck. Two cardboard boxes wait outside Cancer Research. The postman passed. A whistling cockney who wears shorts whatever the weather. But the man on the train seldom receives post. He sent for catalogues for a while. *Boden, Hush.* Beaming couples in cashmere loungewear, angelic families in chunky knits. But it seemed wrong, killing all those trees for paper.

'Hey, *bach*?' A hand on his arm. A woman in a jade-green trilby. She must be 85, if she's a day. Her touch is soothing somehow. He wishes he could ask her to leave her hand there, to press a little more firmly. He tries to hold on to the imprint of her fingers.

'Yes. Yes. I'm fine.' His voice surprises him. It's been several weeks since he spoke aloud to another human.

'Are you cold, love? I've got a blanket you can have?' The lines of her face are blurred, indistinct, but her hair is startling: a halo of sea blue curls beneath the jade. Her mouth the lustrous red of a toothpaste commercial.

'No. No thank you.' He turns away before she can see the tears welling.

*

Jagged convulsions behind his right ribcage, razor edged. Knife-like pain, one of the forums had said. Sitting makes it worse.

He focuses on the names of the stations. Forms them silently in his mind. There was a time when this journey was a constant. A time when…

Birmingham International.

Birmingham New Street.

Smethwick Galton Bridge.

Is this a mantra? Don't think. Start again.

Wolverhampton. *Whampton.*

Telford Central. The ice rink. That cafe where they had ice cream sundaes shaped like swans. Sundae? Sunday?

Wellington.

Shrewsbury.

Welshpool. *Y Trallwng.* As though Welshpool wasn't Welsh enough. No, no.

Birmingham International.

Birmingham New Street.

Smethwick Galton Bridge.

Wolverhampton.

Telford Central.

Shrewsbury. ShREWS-BERRY. ShROSE-BERRY. He had his first kiss in the station yard. Mickey Johnson. She was chewing Wrigley's Juicy Fruit. Those red and yellow packets. She passed it to him mid-snog. Must have had it tucked in her cheek. Tough, over-chewed gum. Her tongue searching for his. First soft, then unexpectedly muscular.

Welshpool.

Newtown.

Caersws.

Machynlleth. Say that after three drinks. No. Start again.

Birmingham International.

Birmingham New Street.

Smethwick Galton Bridge.

Wolverhampton.

Telford Central.

Shrewsbury.

Welshpool.

Newtown. A dingy shop. Mother's Day? No. No... it was Sunday closing in those days. What then? Mum's birthday? *You first. No, you.* A hand on his back. Guffawing. *God there's a right load of cobblers in here. Here, look at this! What's that? A Margaret Thatcher nutcracker, blimey.*

Caersws.

Dyfi Junction.

*

It's too much. He can't be where people are.

Can't sit. Can't stand up.

He sways, staggers, feels the violent urge to piss.

'Excuse me. Excuse me.'

The gangway is packed. Thick air. Hot bodies. Sweet and acrid. Aftershave, sweat, stewed tea, sun cream.

He stumbles into a vast suitcase blocking the aisle. Sky blue with a pattern like clouds. He tastes syrup, red fruit, the memory of last night's wine. His throat swells. He can't help it; he heaves and retches. He steadies himself on the suitcase.

'Do you *mind*?'

'Disgusting.'

'Eeew.'

Stares of righteous indignation brand his skin. There was a time when the looks were different. Admiring. Envious.

A thread of green bile clings to his cheek.

A middle-aged man says something to him. He shakes his head. It's like a silent movie. Or one of those zoom calls. *Can you hear me? I can't hear you. You're on mute.* Silently mouthing at camera.

Too hot. Too hot.

A glass tumbles, water soaks his trainers. *Fancy a dip, anyone?* He has to escape.

He pushes. Uses his elbows. Those bloody train doors that are meant to be automatic. He stabs at the button. His hands are enormous, his fingers won't bend. Is he wearing gloves?

Birmingham International.

His insides tugging, pulling, wrenching.

Birmingham New Street.

Squeezing, tearing.

Wolverhampton.

Toilet. Orange-rimmed sign.

Push to open. Stab.

Telford Central.

Push to close. Stab.

Shrewsbury.

Move lever to lock.

His mouth. The dryness. That smell again. Sweat and sugar.

Caution, very hot water. *It's cooler in the shallows. Come on. Race you!*

He falls back.

Elvis died on the toilet. Judy Garland. That man from *The Sopranos*.

Welshpool.

Is that water? Is the train crossing a river?

A novelty ringtone jangles 'O Sole Mio'.

Aberystwyth.

*

Two boys sprawl on a riverbank. It's peaceful where they are. A bend away from the popular spots where the end of summer's grockles splash in dinghies, shrieking as the coolness of the dappled water meets soft flesh. This place, theirs, is a bank less travelled. A stumble too far from the van with its thin, discordant tune and the gentle-eyed man serving dripping, pink-striped Mr Whippy, and lurid shades of Panda Pops.

Zoom in and they're not boys, but not men either. A childlike softness around the cheeks of one; the other is darker-haired, skin speckled with stubble. His eyes are closed. The first trails his hand through the long grass. It's been hot, but the fronds here remain lush, shaded by overhanging branches of lime and oak, the river close enough to whisper through the trees.

Zoom closer. Notice the smaller of the two. Eager eyed, curious, a glimmer not yet lost. Wait. See the tracing of tightness about his lips? A shadow of silence not yet come. The man on the train. Click. Frozen in time.

He glances at his friend.

'Robbo?' he whispers.

The hint of a smile, a tickle at the corner of his friend's mouth.

'You coming in?' asks the first.

His friend's eyes open a crack. He twists his neck and peers through slits, smile broad and lazy. Heat drunk.

'In a bit.'

He jabs him in the side.

'Ow, Knickers. Bloody hell.'

'C'mon. It's boiling.'

Robbo sighs. Shakes himself like a dog. 'You're a pain. You know that?'

The first boy turns away laughing, pulls down his shorts. He'll go in in his boxers.

Something cold and sticky streams down Knickers's back.

'AAAaargh. Hey! What the—'

Robbo screeches with laughter.

Knickers scrubs at it with his discarded shorts. Something reddish. Raspberry? No. Cherryade.

'You nob-end—'

He whips around, but Robbo's already pelting down the bank towards the river. Knickers chases, whooping and calling, but Robbo's too far ahead. Spare frame, lately sparer, ribs visible at the back, skin tanned dark, peeling at the shoulders. He pauses and watches him – and yes, typical bloody Robbo Morris – he executes a perfect dive. A meticulous arc from bank to river. Enough to make their parents scream. *You'll crack your head. You'll get concussion.* But they're local boys. They know where it's deep enough.

A head pops up, dark curls oily slick. Robbo.

He grins, squinting, hand shading his light-dazzled eyes.

Knickers lurches towards him. He admires his friend's even stroke, but his own flailing style is effective. He dunks Robbo twice for good measure.

Play fighting, semi-real fighting, can't breathe for laughing. They splutter to the surface. Robbo has a single tiny freckle in the corner of one eyelid.

There's a French word: *complice*. No single English word does justice to its meaning. Complicit? Accomplice? The French use it to mean someone who you know so well that they just get you. A tacit understanding, without words, but with words too. An accessory? That doesn't quite do it. A best friend, a lover? A partner in crime, but there doesn't have to be a crime.

'Hey, dreamer. Don't disappear on me.' Real, true, goofy Robbo brings him back.

They float on their stomachs, drifting precariously close to the sharp rocks in the shallows, until they're forced to get up, the clear edges of the water barely covering their feet.

'How about another beer?' Robbo asks.

He hands him a cool one. And something else.

'Happy Birthday, mate.'

An oddly shaped package. Knickers already knows what it is.

Laughing, he places it down beside his towel.

'No… wait… open it,' says Robbo. 'There's something else.'

It's true. There's a bulge at the side of the usual shape.

Robbo's a good wrapper. Knickers starts to say something. *Did your mum help you with this?* But he stops. It's beautiful. Peacock blue, would you call it? Aquamarine? Robbo's even tied a bow around it. Deep jewel green.

He runs the silky smoothness of the ribbon through his fingers.

He picks at the knot until it gives.

A turquoise and jade ceramic pony, short-legged with glossy cherry-coloured lips and spidery eyelashes. A truly hideous item. *Bessie.* A running joke. They've exchanged the same gift for three years of birthdays and Christmases. They found it in this weird little shop, perhaps a little stoned. They were supposed to meet a girl in Shrewsbury, but they got off at Newtown by mistake. The girl was well pissed off. Stone cold blanked his calls after.

Knickers smooths the paper. A cassette falls out. He catches it, turns it over. It's a mix tape. 120 minutes. It must have taken ages. Something's taped on the side. A label: *Robbo and Knickers 1994.*

'This is amazing—'

He clicks it open. There's a playlist. He reads aloud.

'*Parkli—*'

'Don't look at it now… I… it's all our songs. A mega mix. Listen to it later—'

'Okay,' he says.

He lies back in the grass. 'Thanks, Rob. I love it.'

'Knickers?'

He turns to his friend. Robbo's eyes are closed.

'I've been thinking about Bessie,' he says.

Robbo pauses. The silence stretches. Knickers holds his breath. Is this one of Robbo's jokes?

'She's a bit like us. Bessie is.'

He is joking. 'What? Stumpy legs? Worst ride in town?' Sniggers.

Robbo doesn't look at him.

The sky is a fierce burning blue.

'No. I'm serious. Listen… remember when we found her?'

'Scorched in my memory. That woman tried to charge us four quid. *Lovely piece, isn't she? Shall I gift-wrap her for you?* It'll be etched on my gravestone.'

'Not like that… it's Bessie. It doesn't matter how old we are. She'll always be the same.'

'A few more chips maybe? Paint a bit faded.'

'Shh, you're not listening. Bessie… she's like us… if something happened to you. To us. If we left Aber… lost touch… all the things we've done together, they'd still be real. They'd still have happened. Like Bessie. It doesn't matter where you look at us from. The future, or the past. We'll still be friends.'

'I think you're a bit touched, mate.'

Robbo goes quiet again. Has he hurt his feelings?

'Of course, we'll still be friends,' he says. 'And we won't lose touch. London's not that far.'

'No, of course. But that's a perfect example. Imagine you're at Uni. And I'm somewhere else? You take Bessie with you. And because of Bessie, *you know* there's still Robbo. And *I know*

14

there's still Knickers. And somewhere in time, there's Robbo and Knickers and Bessie together.' He's triumphant.

He's nuts, of course, but that's Robbo. A Poundland philosopher.

'Schrödinger's Horse?' Knickers says doubtfully.

'Schrödinger's Horse!' Robbo all but shrieks. He shakes his head, amazed. 'That's it exactly. What would I do without you, Knickers?'

He's beaming. Pleased as punch by his friend's praise. Like a kid with a 99.

They dissolve into guffaws, bent double in the grass, laughing and panting like a couple of loons. Robbo clutches his sides. Every so often one of them sniggers and mutters 'Schrödinger's Horse' and that sets them off again.

Robbo's the first to recover. He props himself on his elbows and sips his warm beer.

'That's something though, isn't it?' he says.

'What's that, Rob?'

He rolls over, so there's barely a centimetre between them, then whispers in Knickers's ear.

'We'll always have Bessie, Knickers.'

He's about to laugh, but before he can, Robbo kisses his cheek. His lips are dry, and he smells of beer, but it's the softest thing he's ever felt. He leans back and smiles, and Knickers can see that tiny freckle. And he can't stop smiling at Robbo Morris because he's right. They'll always share an ugly blue and green china horse.

*

The man on the train doesn't see the two boys. His eyes flicker and come to rest on a wad of toilet roll that some wit has stuck to the ceiling with a vestige of their bodily fluids. He doesn't see that either.

A man on a small, crowded train who wanted to go home.

There is nothing lovely about the way this is ending. No tunnel. No bright lights. No long-lost parent stretching out a reassuring hand. Only a violent rupture which takes the man's lungs, his stomach, and his bowels.

Somewhere, somehow, there is another version of the man – a man who reached the end of the line. A man who woke, in a hospital bed, with a lumpy package on the table beside him. A man who noticed a tiny freckle on the face of a friend. A man who heard someone speak his name aloud. A man who would dip his toes in the cool shallows of a river. A man who might laugh. But that version is fading fast. Now there is only the man on the train, the toilet cubicle, and the vibrations of the rails and joints as the two carriages speed over them.

Colonial Gifts

Alan Bryant

At times of quiet contemplation, such as waiting for the rice to cook, I used to wonder: would I be as true to myself if I lived somewhere less heavenly, in a place of hellfire and avarice, where golden gravy boats have more tone than taste? Would I recognise the predator? Could I bargain with the charlatan, negotiate with the unprincipled pickpockets of morality who trawl without conscience through the lives of others? Is there, coiled in my slumbering naivety, an ability to deceive the deceiver?

Because living on a small island blessed with nature's extravagances can feed our minds with complacency. Here, the air sings to you, invites you to dance to its tune and savour the fruits of slow freedom. It is a gentle melody, pervading the land with mystique. The chorus cuddles up inside you like a lullaby, and the fruits lay sweet on your tongue like your first kiss. The few tourists who find us say we live in a tropical paradise. It is. But to us, this paradise means home.

This timeless jewel is overseen by high, ochre ranges, drowsy guardians of all who have lived, loved and lain here since the earth cushioned the hills with wildflowers and gave us palms to shade under. And my days are fanned by breezes flushed with neighbours' pearly choruses of, 'Hi, Milly, how ya doin today?'

Our town has one street where my father and I keep a café

with some rooms to rent. It's the nearest we have to a hotel. My father is old and weak but does his best to help. All he ever asked of me was a grandchild: but I tell him, being at the stale end of my thirties, unless three wise men arrive following a star, it is unlikely.

Half of our people live within a mile of the town, the rest scatter themselves about the land on small farms. From any hilltop, these homesteads stand out like baize patches on a crumpled cloth. We have some tourists. Most of them are rich, and we treat them with respect and smile for them. It is a sort of commercial courtesy.

One morning, a man arrived on his yacht. His shoes were shiny and white so we knew he would be rich. He was very respectful, an admirable quality, especially for a tourist, and asked to stay with us for a week. At dinner, I served a spiced vegetable casserole with hot bread and my father's cool golden wine. For dessert, I made a layered sponge cake with apricot sauce. This is my speciality. All my recipes are handed down from my mother and her mother before.

He said, 'Milly, I have dined the world over, and this is one of the finest meals I have eaten. And your dessert was superb. After a month at sea, it's the first meal I've had without ketchup.'

I said, 'Thank you, sir, we don't have ketchup on the island, only real food.' And I gave him a big smile, because he was a tourist.

The man, Richard, took out his notebook and wrote something down. He was always writing in his book.

The next day he asked for a taxi to travel around the island. Gerard, the policeman, has the only car, so he drove him for the day. Gerard said the man was very respectful and made lots of notes in his book. Richard probably paid him well too but Gerard is not a man to boast about his income, especially when it is cash in hand. Richard stayed with us for a week, asked questions of everyone and filled up his notebook. On leaving, he gave people large tips, but not to me – I refused. I smiled of course, but anyone who gives money away will always come back with a list of favours they want in return. With tourists, everything has a price.

'Come back and see us again,' the people called to him.

'I will,' he shouted. And he sailed away on his yacht.

*

A month later he returned with two other men and they all stayed in our hotel. They, too, complimented me on my cooking. 'Excellent fish,' they said.

'Thank you,' I said. 'My father caught them today.'

'But there are seeds in these grapes.'

I explained, 'Everything on this Earth must have seeds. How else would we grow food?'

They laughed. Maybe money is attracted to stupid people.

'And you don't have ketchup,' they said. 'That is unusual.'

I said, 'It may be unusual for you, but not for us.'

When they asked about mobile phone signals, I told them, 'We have no phone coverage and no internet or TV.' They laughed again, saying that they would not survive without their mobiles. I said if that was the case, they had better organise their funerals fast, and I smiled. Well, they were tourists.

I said, 'Although we cook on woodstoves, we are civilised. Our main street has electric lighting. Though most think it is unnatural and use oil lamps and candles.'

All week, Gerard drove them around the island in his police

19

car. He said they took photographs and made lots of notes. Wherever they went, young men would ask to sail back to the city with them. They wanted to get rich in their land of gold.

But the visitors told them, 'You have a fine life here. Stay and enjoy your lives in paradise. The city is full of crooks and people chasing money.'

So, I ask myself, why do they go back?

Before leaving, they arranged a banquet on the beach for everyone on the island, including the town council. I took a bowl of stew and a giant sponge cake. From their yacht, they brought cans of food, cases of champagne and of course, ketchup. It was a wonderful day. Except for the ketchup. Richard stood on the table and made a fine speech.

He said, 'This beautiful island should be shown to the world. I could bring a lot of business here with rich tourists.' Then he offered to buy all the small farms for much more money than they were worth, saying he would let the farmers stay on their land and employ them for high wages. They all thought he was a stupid rich man, and after drinking his champagne all day, many decided to take his money.

Soon, surveyors came to check the harbour. They said it was too shallow and would need expanding. The council said that if Richard paid for the construction he could carry on. So, his men blew the old walls apart. The fisherfolk said the explosion killed some fish and frightened the rest away. However, they carried on dredging and blasting to build a larger harbour.

The fish would come back, Richard said, and he offered to buy their boats and pay them good wages to work for him. Of course, the fisherfolk agreed. They thought he was stupid too. I started wondering about this man and his promises. Now he owned most of the island's food production.

With the new harbour, more yachts came, bringing more people and more money. When they went home they told others how beautiful the island was. Bigger ships came with visitors saying they would love to stay here.

*

Richard landed by helicopter one day and convened a meeting with the town council. 'Visitors love it here so much,' he said, 'they want to stay on your island. We should have a proper hotel, then the tourists will spend much more.'

'If you pay for it,' the council said, 'we will agree.'

Soon ships came with heavy machinery for digging foundations. More ships brought skilled workmen and materials to build a huge hotel facing the beachfront.

Some of them stayed with me, but many had to live in tents. At night the workmen got drunk on city whisky and caused trouble in the town. But not in my hotel. My customers knew how to behave. Because I had told them how they must behave. When the council asked Richard to control his workforce, he said the police should do that. But Gerard said he was not experienced with lawbreakers. He was a symbolic token of the law. Anyway, he could not lock them up as we had no jail. So, they kept on drinking and causing mayhem.

When it was finished, they built another hotel, and another. All three hotels faced the beach. But for some reason, they built swimming pools in front of the hotels and moved tonnes of sand from the beach to the pools to make it like an inland seashore. I asked Richard, 'Why do you need swimming pools with sand when we have the beach and the sea to swim in?' He said it was too far to walk to the beach, so he took the beach to the hotels. Once again I questioned the intelligence of these rich people. Then he built high walls around the whole area and fitted gates and security guards.

I wondered if we had been too trusting. He was showing an arrogance I had not seen before. When he next went to the town council, he told them, 'The hotels need more electricity. And we must have mobile phone cover, TV and internet access for the tourists. It is time to build windmills and fill the hills with solar panels.'

'Our hills are painted in flowers,' I said. 'If you destroy them, you will blight our island.'

Richard appeared sympathetic, but the next day his workers bulldozed roads to the hilltops. They covered the hills with panels and windmills, then erected two masts up into the sky. For this, I gave him a piece of my mind. He gave my father and me a phone each and a TV. We will never use them, of course.

It was a year later, when the builders went home, and new people arrived to work in the hotels. 'Now the tourists will come with more money,' Richard said.

He was right. The ships landed and visitors came in their hundreds. The islanders celebrated. 'We will all be rich,' said the councillors. But once the people went into the new hotels, they never came out to the beach or the town. They stayed inside the high walls, reclining by their plastic pools and false beaches.

Richard then told the fisherfolk and farmers they had targets to reach or he would not employ them any more. He said he would bring people from the city to do the work instead. But his targets were impossible. So, he did not pay them and the farmers had nowhere to live and the fisherfolk were without work. This was unforgivable. The man had no respect.

However, he was also having trouble with the hotel staff.

They wanted higher wages. Of course, he said he could not afford to pay more money. Though no one believed him.

He came to me asking if I would help him with the catering in the hotels and said he would pay me well.

I told him, 'I don't want your money. I have enough to do looking after my customers. And my father needs me, he is ill.' That day, Richard sent the company doctor to treat my father and a nurse to care for him. This meant I was obligated to go to the hotel kitchens to help him. But he wanted American food. I tried, but I could not do it. I told him, 'I won't cook this rubbish. People deserve better than this.' So, he was forced to bring in chefs from the city at greater cost.

When I went to the kitchen next, it had transformed into a factory smelling of machinery and scorched meat. I stood, shaking my head, watching conveyor belts of pre-packed meals and burger things. At the end of each belt was a huge, shiny vat of ketchup. There was enough ketchup to fill his swimming pools.

'You cannot serve this,' I said. 'Not even to tourists. They are your guests. You should cook proper food.'

He said, 'Business has to operate at a profit, or it cannot survive. I must get my money back for everything I have done for your island. The tourists will love these burgers.'

I do not know why, but he was right. They plastered their food in ketchup, saying how wonderful it was to have real home-cooked food while on holiday. I told him, 'Your tourists are strange. If they want home-cooked food, they should stay at home with their ketchup.' He did not care.

'I want you to do me a huge favour, Milly,' he said. 'Next week, I'm expecting an important American financier to inspect the hotel. Bake one of your extra special cakes for him. We must do all we can to get the money.'

I shook my head. 'What is this "we"? There is no "we" here. What makes you think I have time to cook for you? I have work to do.'

He pleaded with me. 'But I have borrowed so much to build the hotels. I need to refinance otherwise I will lose everything, and the island will have no tourists. I have told him the hotel is finished. I have cut a few corners on construction and there are some jobs left. But if I can show him the best parts and sit him down with one of your sponges, I know we can get the money.'

'So how can one cake save your hotel?'

'He is a food connoisseur. When I told him about your cakes, he cancelled all his appointments to come here. We can't let him down.'

'I will not do this for you,' I said. But his bottom lip started to judder. A crying man is not pretty and it will always irritate me to see one up close. So, I moved away from him. 'But I will do it for the doctor who helped my father. Because he was a truly kind man.'

*

A week later my new phone rang for the first time. Richard had returned. He was busy inspecting the hotels and false beaches. 'You must show me the cake ready for my financier,' he said. 'Bring it to the hotel now.'

'I have a cheese and potato pie in the oven,' I said. 'It is a natural law that people can wait; cheese and potato pies in ovens cannot. Come here and see it for yourself.' And I put the phone down.

Richard arrived in a breathless rush. Seeing the cake, he stopped, staring wide-eyed. 'Milly, you are a genius.'

'For once you are correct,' I told him. 'There are four rum-drizzled layers of different coloured sponges filled with alternate cream and jellied peaches. I have topped it with a thin layer of banana sauce so as not to overpower the sponge. And let me tell you, this cake is too good for you.'

'It's almost too lovely to eat,' he said.

With that, he pushed his finger down through the centre of the cake and dragged it across to the outside. He held up his finger with the clump of creamy cake balancing on it, gazing at it as if holding a work of art. Then he stuffed it in his mouth and swallowed it. 'Wonderful,' he said. 'Amazing texture.' He had cream all down his silk shirt.

I stood horrified. 'You like the cake?' I said. 'But you have destroyed it.'

'It's fantastic,' he said. 'I love it. Make me another one quickly. This time you had better put one layer of ketchup in it. He'll like that. He owns a burger chain with his own brand of ketchup.'

I had to blink to prove I was not dreaming. He spoke in such an easy disregarding manner without respect for anyone or anything. I was speechless. But for only a few seconds. 'Do you really think I would make you another cake?' I said. 'With your ketchup? I will not defile any food of mine for you or your financial friends.'

I never saw a man change his demeanour so fast. His voice was crying as he spoke. 'Please, I have promised him. You must make another one, please. If I break my word to him he will lose trust in me. Without this finance I will be ruined. Please, you can have anything you want. Make me another cake. Please.'

His eyes began to fill and overflow.

'You have had your cake,' I said. 'Now I have a cheese and

potato pie to attend to. To me, it is more important than you or your money, or your ketchup sponges.'

He clasped his hands together prayerlike. 'But he is expecting it. Desserts are his passion. To him, they are sacred. When he is not financing companies, he bakes, and searches the world for the finest food.'

Richard stood at my kitchen table biting his nails, which normally I would have told him not to. But tears were running down his cheeks.

I pushed him out of the door. 'Don't you dare cry on my vegetables. I have given them enough salt already.' I heard him crying out in the street as he walked away.

At lunchtime, a man entered the café wearing white jeans with a white shirt and shoes even whiter and shinier than Richard's. He ordered a pot of tea. 'Do you have any sponge cake, please?'

He seemed amused as I looked him up and down. 'You must be Mr Burger, the man with his own ketchup company,' I said.

His teeth gleamed white as wedding cakes. 'Please, call me Magnus. I hear you make the best cakes on the island.' Quietly spoken, even his voice smiled.

'No,' I said. 'I make the best cakes in the world.'

He smiled again, a smile that made you want to sit down and talk. He held out his hand in greeting. His skin was soft, and though I felt strength in his handshake when he clasped his other hand lightly around mine there was a tenderness to it.

'Richard is in tears. He said you made a sponge but it didn't turn out right.'

'He told you that? He's got some nerve.'

I went into the kitchen and brought out his tea, and the cake. 'He wanted to try it, so he did – with his finger. He thinks

26

we all owe him so much for turning our island into a nightclub. He has no respect.'

Magnus sat looking at the broken cake and gave a low whistle through his perfectly formed lips. 'May I try a piece, please?'

I cut a slice from the best side and served it on a plate with a spoon. Some people eat cake with a fork but a dessert should be eaten with a spoon. Forks are for meat and vegetables. My mother said that to me. She was never wrong.

He took a full spoonful, let it sit in his mouth until it dissolved. Then he swallowed, waited a minute and took another spoonful. 'This is exquisite,' he said. 'I'd be happy to buy the recipe from you. I would pay you well.'

My hand went to my heart. 'These ingredients are in everyone's cupboard. The only thing I add is love. How can you include that in a recipe?'

He sat eating slowly until his plate was empty. 'He really did that with his finger?'

'I was too surprised to stop him.'

'Well, you're right about this cake deserving respect. Did he ask you to make another?'

'He did and he asked me to put a layer of ketchup in it.'

His eyebrows raised high into his head.

'Ketchup?'

'You Americans seem to have the taste buds of Venus flytraps.'

He smiled again. 'Richard can be excitable at times. Yes, I own a fast-food chain with its own ketchup brand but I wouldn't expect to find any in a dessert, especially of this quality. He needs to cool down.'

'He needs your money, but if he gets it he will turn this island into the devil's circus. He has already thrown the farmers off their land and put the fisherfolk out of work. And he has desecrated our hills with his sun panels.'

'He did all that? Of course, it is a shame to lose any beauty of this island. Possibly they can take some panels away. But the site must have electricity. And I'm sorry about the farmers and fisherfolk. That's unfair.'

I wanted to tell him that Richard should be buried up to his neck in sand and his head covered in honey. But I was brought up to be a fair and compassionate woman. Anyway, it would be a waste of good honey.

'Well, if I may, I'll have another slice of this cake.' He took out his wallet and put some notes on the table.

'There is no need for money.'

'Please, keep it, and make me another if you would.'

'With or without ketchup?'

Another smile showed his wedding-cake teeth once more and he shook his head. 'Preferably without. When can you bake it?'

His voice had the consistency of soft cream. In my mind, I was setting strawberries into his every word. I rose from my chair. 'For you, Magnus, I will start straight away.'

'May I watch you make it, please, Milly?'

His face shone with such cheeky expectation, I had to smile back at him. More than soft cream, his tone had a way of entering my ears and filtering through my body. It was an odd, not unpleasant experience, one I had not felt for many years. Strangely, when I went to answer, the words were hovering in my throat like lost butterflies. I took a deep breath. 'You're welcome to stay, Magnus. We'll bake it today, and if you want, you can call over in the morning to help me layer it. My mother taught me how to make this sponge, as her mother taught her.'

He rose from his chair. 'Okay, Milly, let's bake a cake.'

The kitchen breathed scents of new bread and cinnamon, and he watched as I mixed the ingredients.

His level of empathy was rare for a man. He knew what to say and how to ask a question without it being too direct or personal, even though it might be. He showed interest in my life on the island, my childhood, my father, my dreams for the future. I told him I had never left here and would never want to. Why would I?

He sighed. 'Your life is so peaceful, Milly. The new hotel is a busy, raucous place day and night. Do you have a room to spare for a few days, please?'

When my father came home with his fish, Magnus shook his hand. I could see he was impressed by this man and he looked at me with a glint in his eye that asked if Magnus and I were becoming more than friends. I admit there were moments when I wondered about that too.

I'm sure he knew the power his gaze held. I surely knew. Sometimes, he would look at me with his smiling eyes and I was seventeen again. Long-forgotten feelings ran through my mind and my body. At my age, I should be ashamed to say these things, but my barriers began to melt away like warm butter in a pan. It was not as if the man, this lovely man, gave direct compliments, or flirted. He spoke to me as a friend who was interested in me, wanting to find out who I was, what I looked for in life, and why. In less than a few hours that afternoon, his presence became a gentle, understated refreshment to my emotions. He was a breeze lifting me up to waltz through my clouded barriers of fear and distrust.

As a teenage girl in love, I dreamt of having a family. Zac was beautiful, but he wanted more than the island could give. One day, as so many young men have done, he stepped onto a boat and sailed for the mainland. I could have gone with him but girls did not do that. We stayed at home waiting. And waiting. Zac did not say he would get rich and return for me. He did not promise anything.

Why do we expect so much of those who make no promises to us? Why are we so disappointed when those promises not made do not happen as we wish them to? I began to wonder what promises Magnus would not make.

He rarely went to the hotels. Some days, Gerard would drive him around the island and he would chat to the farmers. Or he would sail out in the bay on the fishing boats. If we spent time together in the kitchen, he would talk of his business interests across the continents. After setting them up, he assigned someone to oversee them, he said. He delegated everything so he would have more time to travel.

*

At the end of the week, he said, 'I shall be leaving in a few days. I have taken ownership of the hotel and Richard has gone home. The farmers and fisherfolk will have their land and boats returned to them. They can repay their debt by supplying produce to the hotel.'

The evening before he left, we sat in the garden drinking wine. Aromas of juniper and herbs floated hand in hand through moonlit air spangled with fireflies. We talked until late, then he rose, thanked me, and rested his cheek on mine. His mouth touched my face with a kiss that alluded to warm friendship, and perhaps more, or possibly not. Who could tell?

I was unable to move. I seemed to freeze and melt simultaneously. Then he went to his room and I went to mine. But I did not sleep. I imagined him lying in his bed waiting for me to go to him. But was I mistaken? He might not have had the same feelings for me. But what if he did? What if I tried to open his door and it was locked? He might wake and what would he think of me? Or would it be unlocked? Was he waiting for me? Or what if he was queer?

Heart thumping in my throat, I touched his door handle, pressing it down gently. My guilt whirlpooled into disappointment. His door was locked. I tried to turn and leave but could not. My fingers glued themselves to the metal. Against my every instinct, my hand started to push down on it again. Then I heard the click of the lock, and slowly he opened the door. We did not speak. He held out his arms. I must have floated to him. With feelings of relief and safety, my body melted into his embrace. His arms eased me to him, his lips travelling round my face with the lightest pressure until finding my mouth. Emotions transcended love, romance, or sex. I was enfolded in a quilted haven of shelter.

In the morning, we breakfasted together, chatting about his return trip. Then he kissed my cheek with that same tenderness, and he left. I could have asked him, but he would not have stayed. He has his life of business and travel, with its constant feed of projects filtering through his mind. And my life is here.

Though it is difficult to define, everyone has ideas about what love is, be it lifelong or fleeting. To some, love means being at someone's side no matter what the consequences. This is not always possible. To me, the question is, when it happens should we grasp it whatever the consequences? For that week, I loved Magnus. That was enough.

*

It has been one year since that time. Today I was in the garden picking herbs when my father called to me from the house.

'Milly, you must come and see this,' he said. He was watching the advertisements on TV. He prefers them to the programmes, which he says are either politicians telling lies or game shows giving prizes people do not need. 'Look,' he said.

On the TV screen were pictures of small boxes, pink and blue, thousands of them on conveyor belts. When the camera moved in closer, inside each box was a four-layer cream and fruit sponge. 'Mother's sponge cakes deserve respect,' the voice-over said. 'This might be the finest tropical island dessert in the world.'

Again, I was surprised that someone with his love of high-quality food would treat others with such disdain as to feed them by mass production. Yes, Magnus is a lovely man but his priority will always be business. To him, it was only natural he should profit from my baking. I was under no illusions about his intentions. But I am a fair and compassionate woman, and sometimes, to be fair to ourselves, we must hold out our hands in the joyous belief that the dream nestling asleep in our palms will be kissed by the magic of chimeric moonbeams. So, I went to his room. He could take what he wanted from me, but as a businessman, he would know everything has its price. However, he could not realise the true value of my reimbursement.

I looked into the small cot sitting at my father's side. My baby was wide awake, listening to the sound of his father's sales pitch on the television. When he grows, I will tell him his daddy was a beautiful man – for a tourist.

Fern Baby

Natalie Ann Holborow

Charlotte knew there was something special about the fern. She put down the tray of lobelia flowers she was carrying and reached out to rub at the fern's spray of fronds.

'I'll take this too,' she told the woman at the cash register.

'Good choice,' said the woman.

'How old?' Charlotte pointed at the fern sitting between them.

The woman raised an eyebrow, then shrugged. 'Never asked it.'

In the car, Charlotte pulled the seat belt carefully around the pot, mint-green and immaculate.

'So that you're safe,' she whispered to the fern. She didn't even light up a cigarette for the drive home; she didn't want any toxins to be absorbed by the leaves.

She knew about passive smoking.

*

Charlotte named the fern Frida, like Frida Kahlo. She decided this on the drive home.

When she arrived outside the house, a small bungalow that overlooked the estuary, she was careful to carry Frida with great care. She even slowed her breathing, as though breathing too hard might blow her out of her arms and onto the drive.

James, her neighbour, was standing outside his front door, balancing a cigarette between his lips. He always looked like he had just woken up, even though it was three in the afternoon. His dressing gown was open over an Iron Maiden T-shirt and he wasn't wearing any shoes.

'New plant?' he called when he saw Charlotte. He had the sprinklers on again. They spun wide, sparkling circles over the lawn.

'Yes. This is Frida.' Charlotte stroked a finger over the pot protectively.

James pulled on his cigarette and exhaled, his face briefly disappearing behind the smoke. 'You always name your plants?'

'Only this one.'

'Sound,' he said. James had a lot of plants himself, but they were kept under very specific conditions and he didn't like to talk about them. Sometimes, on summer evenings with the windows open, Charlotte could smell them. She was sure most of the street could, but no one ever said anything; it wasn't that kind of neighbourhood.

'Well, if you ever want a plant-sitter, I'm right next door.'

Charlotte smiled at him and pulled Frida into her chest more tightly. 'I don't think I'll ever leave her long enough to need one.'

James gave her what might have been a smirk, but she wasn't sure. 'Yeah, thought so.'

Charlotte adjusted Frida one more time, gave James a nod and walked inside, feeling his gaze on her back until the door was shut. She placed Frida on the kitchen windowsill, above the sink. It was an old thing with brass taps and deep enough even to wash a baby in. But this felt wrong, too exposed. More to the point, what kind of mother lets their child sleep in a cold kitchen?

She put the kettle on, tugged her cardigan off the back of the chair and wrapped it around her, rubbing her hands together for warmth. No, the windowsill wasn't going to do. She needed to find a better spot, somewhere warm and light.

*

At first, she thought maybe Frida was being polite, tolerating the new spot the way a guest tolerates an uncomfortable armchair. But after a few days, the fronds that had dropped a little perked up again, brilliantly green. In the mornings, Charlotte would turn to the bedside table and check her soil, pressing her fingers tenderly into the dirt like a doctor checking for a pulse. Too dry and she would give her water from her own glass. Too damp and she'd apologise for loving her too fiercely.

Charlotte spent hours on the bed, glancing up at the fern as she read facts from her laptop. She downloaded PDFs, watched videos, searched Google Images for the biggest ferns she could find, their fronds spreading out like strange fins. She learned that ferns were one of the oldest plants on earth, older than dinosaurs, which she found overwhelming. She learned that they were excellent air purifiers, which she was delighted to discover; all the more proof that Frida needed to be there. They were looking out for each other.

She also read that some people say ferns are a sign of life pushing forward, over and over again, representing the divine cycle of birth, death and rebirth. Something about this made her cry.

One morning, James saw Charlotte cradling Frida in her arms as she watered her. She was outside on the patio, watching the birds drop for seed and then lift again, their dark wings sharp against the sky's blank ledger. James had been in his shed. He glanced up quickly at the CCTV camera attached to the back of his house, pointing directly at where he was standing.

Charlotte had read that speaking to plants helps them grow, so she was telling Frida about her childhood in Brecon, about how the damp winds off the edges of mountains sometimes sounded like dismantled music. She told Frida too about the sheep that would stare at her, mid-mouthful, their coats pearled with morning dew.

James squinted at her over the low fence. 'You all right over there?'

Charlotte nodded. 'Just taking care of my daughter. She's growing well, look.' Charlotte tipped the fern towards him to show just how high the tips of her leaves reached.

James made a sound that was somewhere between a laugh and a grunt. He lit up a cigarette and inhaled, talking at the same time so that his voice sounded choked. 'I used to have a cactus,' he said. 'But I drowned it.'

Charlotte looked down at Frida and stroked her pot, the rim cool against her fingers. 'Oh, I won't let that happen.' She looked over at James's shed. 'Your plants are doing all right though?'

James frowned, grunted and walked off. He slammed the door after him, leaving a cloud of smoke dissolving in the space where he'd been, as though he'd just teleported.

*

By the end of the month, Frida was enjoying the light that came through Charlotte's study window. Charlotte liked having her there, where she could see her as she wrote articles, replied to emails and secretly worked on her novel in work hours. Sometimes, if she was on a virtual call, she'd pick Frida up and make her say hello to all the bewildered faces on her laptop screen.

During lunchtimes, Charlotte set a place for Frida at the table: a tiny plate with rabbits on and a little cup. She didn't actually put any food on the plate – she wasn't insane – but she liked the symmetry of it. She sat opposite Frida and chatted about nothing, scraping couscous and little jewels of pomegranate around her plate with a fork.

One afternoon, Charlotte's sister Helen called during lunch and asked if she was 'still seeing that guy… what was his name again? Nick?'

'No,' Charlotte said, placing a damp sheet of kitchen roll around Frida's base like a bib. 'It didn't work out.'

'Are you seeing anyone now?'

'No. I have Frida now.'

There was a long silence. Helen asked, 'You're dating a girl?'

'No. Frida is a fern.'

Charlotte could hear her sister taking a deep breath. 'Like… a houseplant?'

'She's more than that.'

'Okay.' In the background, Helen's two boys were shouting, probably punching each other on the floor. Helen worked from home three days a week, but she didn't particularly enjoy it.

'You wouldn't understand anyway.'

'Okay.'

Charlotte hung up before she could say anything else.

*

On Saturdays, Charlotte took Frida for walks. She carried her in a little sling fashioned out of an old baby carrier she found on Facebook Marketplace. No one really noticed, and if they did, they didn't say anything. Charlotte had read that plants really thrived in fresh air, that it made them stronger. She really wanted Frida to grow up strong.

It was in the park, one day in late July, that she bumped into Nick.

She spotted him sitting on a bench, flipping through some paperback without really reading it. He had that look on his face that people got when they wanted to look like they were waiting for something, but really they weren't. When he saw Charlotte he smiled, a huge, genuinely beaming smile which he then immediately tried to make smaller. He didn't want her to think he'd missed her too much.

'Charlotte,' he said, brushing imaginary dust off his jeans and standing up. 'Wow.'

'Hi.' She stopped a few feet away, close enough to feel the breeze licking her fringe back, but not close enough to feel anything else.

Nick glanced at the sling, at Frida's tiny green fronds poking out. 'Um...?' He nodded at it.

'This is Frida,' said Charlotte, pulling the sling down so Nick could see more clearly. 'She's my daughter.'

Nick gave a confused laugh, but then saw Charlotte wasn't joking. He nodded slowly. 'Right.'

They stood there in silence for what felt like minutes, but it couldn't have been more than a few seconds. Behind them, a duck cackled then plunged its head into the water. There were children aiming rolled-up bits of bread towards it and they shrieked every time it gobbled one up.

'You look good,' he said. 'I like the new fringe.'

She smiled, just barely. 'Thanks.'

Nick nodded at the sling. 'So this... is this a new thing, then?'

'What, the sling? No, I got it on Marketplace.'

'No, Charlotte, the plant.'

'Oh.' Charlotte ran a hand over Frida's leaves, stroking them like they were curls on a child's head. 'We found each other. She needs me.'

A cyclist zipped between them, jingling a bell. Just across the path, two little girls were squealing and releasing a ball into the air, watching as it sailed above them like a pink sun.

Charlotte looked at Nick, really taking him in. His jumper was soft and slightly wrinkled, the collar stretched just enough to suggest that he'd had it a long time. Charlotte was sure she'd seen that jumper before, but she couldn't quite remember any more. Maybe it was the one she used to borrow and pull over her knees, which would explain the baggy collar. His face looked tired, like he hadn't slept much in a long time.

'I used to think about it a lot,' said Nick. 'I used to think about you. How much you wanted that.'

Charlotte inhaled through her nose. 'Well now I have it. We have to go now, don't we, Frida?'

She secured the plant tightly in its sling and looked at Nick. 'Well. Nice seeing you. Take care, Nick.'

'Take care, Charlotte. And… uh… nice meeting you, Frida.'

Nick had never looked so sad as he did then, watching Charlotte walk away with her arms clutched tightly around the fern.

*

Charlotte suspected Nick had reached out to Helen straight after seeing her, because the next day Helen asked her to meet for coffee. Helen was never able to meet for coffee usually. Her boys took up the majority of her energy.

Charlotte got to the cafe with Frida strapped to her chest, her fronds bouncing slightly with each step. She hadn't seen James for a couple of days but knew he was at home because she could smell him smoking, hidden somewhere in the garden. She'd had to keep her windows closed all week and it was nice to be out somewhere she could breathe properly.

Helen was already at a table outside, stirring her coffee over and over, as though she were waiting for something to surface. Her hair was pinned up neatly and her lips were red. She looked striking with her black hair all pulled back like that, like a ballerina. When she saw Charlotte, she smiled. It didn't quite reach her eyes.

'Wow,' she said. 'Look at her.'

'I know, she's really thriving,' Charlotte said, sitting down carefully and lifting Frida out of her pot like she was presenting a newborn. 'She loves being out in the fresh air.'

Helen reached out and ran a fingertip over Frida's leaves. 'She's soft,' she said. 'Delicate.'

'She's still very young.'

Helen let out a breath through her nose, almost like a laugh but smaller. Then she said, 'Of course.'

A waitress came by and looked curiously at Charlotte. 'Would you like me to…'

'No, it's fine, she's not eating,' said Charlotte, nodding at the fern. 'Just a flat white for me, please.' The waitress looked momentarily baffled then nodded, taking the order inside on a tiny notepad.

Helen tilted her head. 'So, what's new?'

'I've moved her to my desk now,' said Charlotte. 'She likes watching me work. I think she's absorbing the creative energy.'

Helen let out a barely audible sigh. So, Nick had been right. 'And what are you working on?'

'Articles for home magazines mostly,' she said. 'I'm doing a plant feature. Frida might even appear in this issue. Isn't that right, Frida?' She made a motion as though she was trying to tickle the plant. It bristled in the wind.

Helen gave a small, polite nod like she didn't know what to do with the words Charlotte had given her. She was still stirring circles into her coffee. 'I always knew you'd be a writer. Even when we were kids.'

Charlotte smiled, still stroking Frida. 'I know it sounds crazy. But she's sparked something in me. I've never felt so creative.'

The waitress slid the coffee over to Charlotte, looking sideways at the plant.

This was worse than Helen had imagined. 'You'd always had a brilliant imagination. Always narrating things, like you were David Attenborough or something, even if we were just making sandcastles.'

Charlotte blew on her coffee and took her first sip. Strong, just how she liked it. Yes, she used to do that. Still did, actually. There was a little voice in her head, always telling the story. *Charlotte lifts her coffee, exhales. Her mouth leaves a berry-coloured imprint on the mug. Charlotte rearranges the fern's leaves so they look more alert, more alive.*

Helen was watching her.

'You're happy though, Charl?' Helen asked. Her voice was careful, like she was testing the weight of the question before saying it.

Charlotte straightened Frida's fronds again, unnecessarily. 'Of course I am.'

On the table beside them, two elderly ladies were leaning in and out to speak, punctuating what they were saying about someone they both knew. Their eyes widened. They had the same haircut and matching handbags. Charlotte wondered if they were sisters, partners or just very close friends.

'I just think,' Charlotte said suddenly, 'people give up on things too easily. You see it though, don't you? They get excited about something, and then when it's inconvenient or messy or not exactly the way they expected, they just...' she made a vague, sweeping motion with her free hand '...throw it away. Move onto whatever else excites them for a bit.'

Helen looked straight at Charlotte. 'Is that what you think happened?'

Charlotte felt like someone was tightening a screw slowly in the side of her jaw. 'Maybe. I think people handle loss differently.' She set her coffee down and felt an unbearable pressure swelling behind her ribs, like a balloon that was filling up too fast, filling up space it had no room for.

'God, Charlotte, are you okay?'

'I'm fine,' she said. The elderly ladies next to them were smearing cream and jam over scones, arguing over the correct order in which to do it. 'What did Nick say to you?'

'Nick?'

'I know he spoke to you. I saw him yesterday.'

Helen sighed. There was no point in lying to Charlotte. 'He said he was worried about the way you were... you know...' she nodded at the fern '...the way you were carrying that plant about and calling it your daughter.'

Charlotte closed her eyes. She'd stopped stroking Frida's leaves and stared out across the estuary. She was watching wild ponies drag their hefts up the salt marsh, heavy with foal, sucking their hooves free from the mudflats as they moved.

'He said he'd have been less worried if you'd instead said you were helping that neighbour of yours grow marijuana plants,' said Helen. 'Look, you're doing a good job with her.'

She reached over and touched the plant. Charlotte flinched. 'But here's the thing. We always think there's this one thing we have to achieve to be fulfilled. But we don't. And I don't know whether I should say this…'

Charlotte gazed at her shoes. 'Go on.'

'…but given the choice, I know I'd have had a fulfilled life even without my boys. I never believed it before them, and now I've got them, I love them more than life itself. I wouldn't trade them for the world. But I'm just saying… it's not everything. You can still have a full life. You can follow what you want to do and that's okay.'

Charlotte looked down at Frida, at the lime-green lattice of fronds, the elegant curve of her stems. She wanted to give so much of herself to this. Her care, her worry, her love. If she let go, if she even so much as loosened her grip slightly, what would she have left?

Her hands tightened around the pot. 'I'm not ready for that.'

Helen reached for her sister's hand and held it. It felt awkward and oddly huge, like a fish had just landed in Charlotte's hand, but she held it there anyway. 'I know.'

Charlotte had known this. She'd known it was coming, ever since she first clipped the seat belt around the pot; ever since she'd first pressed her fingers into Frida's soil; since she tucked her into the sling; since she'd called her *daughter* and felt something settle into her chest, filling a space that had been rattling, hollow, for months.

The thing inside her pressed harder, pushing up, demanding all her space. She looked at Frida again, at the life she was nurturing, at the tiny little miracle that kept on growing in response to her care.

She closed her eyes for a second. And then, just barely, she nodded.

Last Words

Jonathan Page

There is only peace, no thought, on waking. His dressing gown has fallen open and his skin is pleasantly tight with cold. He likes the charcoal delta of the tree stretched and swaying over the yellow ceiling. The on and off again song of a robin in the garden. The sight of his chest and belly rising and falling.

Why is he on the sofa? He touches his head: no headache. There is no glass or bottle on the coffee table. He swings his feet off the armrest and sits up. When he puts out his hand he finds a book, the pages concertinaed and a little torn; a novel, one of his own. Pieces of torn paper, his usual bookmarking technique, drop onto his thighs when he opens it. He tries to decipher the red scrawl, his own awful writing, in the margins. Perhaps he was thinking of a sequel, but he cannot remember anything about last night, cannot remember reading, or making notes, or the idea that must have prompted him.

Breathe.

Listen to the robin, the watery burst and stop of his song.

He has been working too hard, that is all, spent too much time on his own. It will come to him, what he did, and why, after coffee.

It is an old house, renovated, subtly, by an architect friend. The wide, high picture window at the end of the polished elmwood floor prompts him to seek out his name, what he looks like; but if he cannot even remember last night, why try? Don't try.

Don't worry yourself. He walks towards the bare brown hills and the dark line of the oak wood and the perfect maths of the stone wall at the end of the rose garden.

Coffee, coffee, coffee.

The kitchen is a slab of white-veined marble, stone pavers, a converted black range. A large abstract painting, scrambled, piled oils, reproduces the hills he sees in the window. He leans on the kitchen island – a pitted butcher's block set in a rusted steel frame – while his coffee burbles on the hob. Such a great smell. He is at peace again; today is important, not yesterday. He holds the pregnant curve of his belly and wriggles his comic, prehensile toes and pours the coffee into a giant blue mug and sniffs at it and dips his tongue into the scalding liquid and grins and carries the mug back to the front room.

Coffee, then work. No need to dress.

His study is at the end of a long, bowed, lime-washed corridor, one storey up. There is a gentle electric humming somewhere – he stops to listen. The humming stops: it must be his ears, middle age. He pulls his dressing gown tight about him. It would be good to remember why he ended up on the sofa. It will come to him.

Books line the shelves, real ones, novels and poetry and art. There are laws against printing books now, and a kind of fake paper that perfectly reproduces the experience, page after page softly materialising on its surface. Not that anyone reads books much any more, even his books. It is a dwindling, eccentric activity, kept alive by a few enthusiasts and academics, older people, those who remember what it was like before truly immersive VR. He cannot believe reading will ever quite die out though. Boethius must have felt the same before his execution, that same mix of apocalyptic thinking and hope that the word would survive somehow. And it did, it did. It was never really in danger.

So write then, keep going. Keep the faith. He sits down at his desk, a polished sheet of walnut on thin chrome legs, and the transparent screen turns solid with his half-finished manuscript. This novel, his last possibly, his masterpiece possibly, is the work of years. He scrolls to the start of the chapter and reads back what he has written and removes a word and repastes it again and is pleased by what he reads. He types a new sentence – it feels familiar to him. He searches the manuscript and finds the same sentence, one very like, only two chapters ago. He deletes the new sentence, tries again. This too is familiar. He searches, finds it in the second paragraph of the very first chapter. He deletes it and sips his coffee.

The window overlooks a sheep-shorn meadow that slopes gently then steeply down to the stream. The water glimmers under the trees. How does the story go on, where does it go now? Perhaps this impasse is what drove him to his old work yesterday.

He looks at the grey drag of rain in the distance, the delicate stub of rainbow over the lit woods. Do not panic, the words will come, they always have, for decades. The miracle of them is what keeps his agent – he fumbles for her name too – in business. He is the miracle, the aberration, the exception to the rule. No false modesty now, no angst either. Perhaps he should rest today, be content with where he has got to and let the story manifest in dreams, in visions, as it used to.

He puts down his coffee. The sky is turning slate, the meadow a darker, richer green. I do not dream any more.

What is a dream?

Humming again, stronger now: the manuscript vanishes

and the desk light clicks out. At the same moment he seems to see, out of the corner of his eye, a pin of red light appear and disappear where the stream leaves the property. He stares down at the immobile white water and listens to the distant moan of the weather in the window and does not see it again. It was the tiny indicator light on his keyboard reflected in the pane and the coming storm must have shorted the power. These are reasonable explanations. There is something wrong.

He hasn't had breakfast is what is wrong. And strong coffee, though he loves it so, always makes him anxious. The desk light comes on, the white highlights under the keys and the red indicator. So go make toast, fry some fake bacon. A scoop of avocado would be nice, a little lemon, a little pepper. There is a firm pat on the window, a short gap, another pat, a shorter gap: pat pat pat pat until the spread islands of rainwater connect and obliterate the view. He puts his coffee cup to his lips and finds it empty.

*

There is no bread in the bread bin, which is very clean, crumbless, as if there has been no bread in it for a long while, and no veggie bacon in the immaculate, near empty fridge. There are no avocados in the bowl either, no fruit at all, though he clearly remembers bananas and avocados and a single bruised apple from the orchard. He must have eaten it all, or most of it, and cleared the rest out yesterday; he has a tendency to tidy when he gets stuck. He opens the freezer compartment and pulls out half a loaf of plastic-wrapped sliced white bread. Horrible, but it will do. He puts on a second bad-for-me-I-shouldn't pot of coffee.

The garden wall shines under the trees, which shake their

large, rounded heads very slowly, as if a monster was about to appear. There is a slant rake of black lines where the blue-black clouds give way to grey and a short section of drained blue sky. The kitchen window is sunk deep into the house and the rain hardly touches it. There is the dry stone skirting and there is the wet stone skirting just beyond.

The light red earth of the trimmed rose-less rose bushes is bloodier, and more solidly present for the rain. He pats at his dressing gown pockets for the notebook which is not there and hopes to remember the images until he is back at his desk. Novels, his novels anyway, are made of such moments. He has always downplayed plot; it feels more real to him, truer to life, to have his stories delta into other stories and those stories delta into others.

Without thinking, he takes his coffee and the third slice of toast held between his teeth into the front room, instead of back up the stairs, as he had meant to do. The framed photographs on the heavy stone mantel move as he approaches: the teenage girl shakes the long black hair from her face. The older woman holds a black kitten up to the lens. The writer puts his coffee down and kisses his forefinger and touches each photograph in turn. Nothing terrible has happened to his family; they are away, that is all, visiting friends, or working, but their repeated movements, the way his partner hugs and lifts and hugs and lifts the long-dead kitten, make the women seem vulnerable to him. When he has time to sift through the cloud he will replace the pictures with still ones. He goes back to the sofa and eats his toast.

Endless Love.

That is the title of the book. The critics said it sounded like a romance – though what else could he have called it? The novel is a love story. He presses the squeezebox pages together and watches them jack slowly apart. Opens the book at random and reads sentences that seem startlingly similar to those in his current project. Had he read it for inspiration then, or to avoid plagiarising himself, as he pushed forwards?

Perhaps a little of both. The sentences impress him, it is hard to believe that he wrote them, though that too is often the way with writing.

'That is often the way with writing.'

He speaks to the vanishing sweat ring on the coffee table where he lifted away his mug. He sips his coffee, scratches the grey tuft of his beard, sighs, smiles.

'Okay. Well. Perhaps a little of both.' As if an interviewer sat opposite.

'Yes, this one is a love story too, or close enough. A bit darker though. There's death this time, lots of death.'

Interesting. This might get him going: automatic talking instead of automatic writing. Pretend you are answering an interviewer.

'It doesn't matter what the questions are.'

If he were still teaching, if there were any creative writing students left to teach, he would try this technique out on them. He leans forward and his partner offers him, flickeringly, a dead kitten.

*

A male face in a blue hood appears on the wall, the picture blurred and faintly rainbowed with rain. A giant grey eye and a freckled brown nose as the visitor leans into the camera. *Doctor Frank James. Literary Historian. University of Lampeter. 10.30 appointment. Open door?* The nose is subtitled. He waves at the mute symbol and the doorbell repeats the same words in a Welsh-accented female voice. He hasn't had a visitor in a long time; his partner must have booked him and not told him or told him and he had forgotten. God, he isn't even dressed.

'Hello there.'

'Hello.'

The man steps back into the bright white rain, a blue pillar.

'You've caught me in my night things. Let me get some clothes on.'

Door opening. Welcome, Doctor Frank James.

'What…'

The door has taken his flapped sleeve for permission. Doctor James walks into the camera – the writer sees the shoulder of his blue coat then a faint, reaching blue shadow in the porch. There is a choked intake of breath and the scuff and echo of the man's shoes in the hall. A hand appears and disappears in the doorway to the living room.

'Should I take my shoes off?'

'Yes, please. Though whatever you like.'

'I'll take them off.'

The man laughs, abruptly, a kind of gasp.

'Sorry.'

'What for?'

'Your voice. I've lived with that voice for years, decades possibly. All those interviews you gave, back in the day. I never thought… extraordinary.'

The writer wraps the dressing gown more tightly about his body – there is no belt. He holds it in place with his left arm, then the underside of his belly when he rolls back, hard, onto the sofa. But he should offer the man coffee at least. He stands again, hunched to protect his modesty, his baggy blue boxers from view. The man steps into the doorway, extends his hand.

'I left the coat by the mat, I hope that's all right. I couldn't see a hook.'

But there is an antique coat rack in the porch, an unused bamboo cage for umbrellas. Or there was. His partner again, moving things. Not telling him things.

Never asking. Doctor James lowers his forgotten hand and tucks the tips of his fingers in the key pocket of his jeans. He is a decade or so younger than him: slim, muscular, a touch of grey in his close-cropped hair.

'Of course, of course. Listen, how rude. I'm not dressed, as you can see. And you... so smart. Coffee? I can offer you coffee?'

No answer. The click of the visitor's glasses as he unfolds them, puts them on, and turns, and turns, his mouth a little O.

'Amazing.'

The half-whisper of one visiting a church.

'The dressing gown, the pictures. They're real?'

'I'll have a top-up if you're having one.'

'Sorry. Yes. Coffee would be lovely.'

'I don't have any milk, I'm afraid. We're a dairy-free household.'

The visitor lifts the palm of his hand, smiles, turns his back to him.

'As it comes then.'

Odd man. Though who was he to judge, shuffling away, near naked, in his scruffy gown? He was probably just a little star-struck. The coffee jug is still half full; he pours the lukewarm coffee into clean cups and zaps them in the microwave. The hum was artificial, he'd read, or heard – customers weren't convinced their microwaves were working properly, despite the light and timer, so they added a recording of the sound microwaves used to make. But the cups go round, and the hum fits the mechanical action, the tiny spark and ting of the microwaved cups – gold rimmed, a mistake – so perhaps the sound is real after all. He knows so little of the world. He is an antique, like one of those great Victorians, Forster or Russell, who lived on into the Space Age.

'Here you go, Doctor James.'

'Please, call me Frank.'

'Call me Andrew.'

The visitor lowers himself, cautiously, into the lounge chair, as if it were something special, clasps and unclasps its blonde wood arms.

'Forgive me, Andrew. You must think me a bit weird. It's like a dream, really like a dream, meeting you in person.'

Star-struck then. Good.

'I'm only a flabby old man, Frank. It's nice to have a visitor. I hardly get any these days.'

A red light, centred in a transparent clip, pulses on the visitor's belt.

'What is that thing? I'm so behind on tech.'

'This? Not mine. A pass, that's all, to get onto the property.'

'There's only a stone stile down there.'

Frank wipes his chin with his hand, smiles. Looks away at the pictures over the mantel, the shelves of first editions.

'It must be new. My partner told me about it, I expect, and I forgot, as usual. You'd think a writer would listen more to others. Would remember what they told him.'

'Nonsense, I don't believe you, Andrew. You were always – you are – such an empathetic writer, you know. You observe things, people, how they talk, so closely.'

He points at the bookshelf.

'One example. The famous scene, in *Endless Love*, where you describe an argument, a tiff really, between the lovers. You capture it so perfectly, her voice, the narrator's, the tenderness that underlies their frustrations.'

And he remembers the passage, word for word, as Frank references it. He mouths the words over his cup, inaudibly at first, then speaks them out loud, three pages of dialogue, his eyes closed. The squashed paperback is under his knuckles as he repositions himself on the sofa.

'Wow.'

Frank puts the palms of his hands together and dips his head.

'Just wow.'

'You were lucky, I'm not sure I could have done that with any other of my books. I was reading *Endless Love* last night, making notes, for the next one.'

'*Aspects.*'

'Yes, that's the working title. But how could you know that?'

Frank puts his fist over his mouth. The writer sees the bluish imprint from his hand, a thumb print, a scatter of crumbs from his toast on the glass table. His purplish knees and the pale, near hairless spread of his thighs.

'Ah of course. She told me it was good. What there was of it.'

'So far.'

'Yes. So far.'

Frank sets his cup, click, on the low table.

'I've written papers on all ten of your novels, you know. The nine you completed plus the AI novella.'

'That AI thing, that hardly counts. I'm ashamed I took the money.'

'Opinion has changed on that. A lot, actually. It's still you, in a way, your methodology, your voice. You were ahead of your time.'

Were. The past tense again; the AI novella only came out

last year, a stopgap to please the fans. He snatches up the ballooning paperback and slides it across the table. It's four – no – five years since he published *Five Ways*. That used to be nothing. The world moves so fast these days, faster and faster.

'I'm proudest of the books I've actually written. I'm happy to talk about those.'

'Noted.'

Frank claps his palms together. Sniffs the tops of his fingers.

'Let's start again. At the beginning. See if I can do better… *Angels*, your first book. It was semi-autobiographical, right? You grew up near Port Talbot.'

The visitor really does know his novels. The more they talk, the more he likes Frank. And it surprises him how easily he recalls whole passages from his books, doesn't muddle characters, or situations, as he remembers doing at festivals and readings in cold village halls. He quotes, and quotes, and quotes, sees the pages turn, the shadowed cleft between the pages, the changes in font and font size and paper quality. *Five Ways* came out after the law changed. But he even sees the grey-tinged fake paper, how each page magically fades away and replaces itself as the eye reaches the footer.

The fat ochre floor lamp switches itself on, a dim orange light that illuminates only itself and a small slant oval of carpet.

'It's getting late, I didn't click.'

'I've kept you from your work.'

'No, you haven't, Frank, it's been a pleasure. A privilege even.'

And it was, it is, having him here, listening, barely interrupting him, once he got going.

'I never do this, not with a first draft, but, you know, would you like to see it? *Aspects* I mean. My writing room.'

*

Andrew stands at the window while Frank sits at the desk, his face and hands skinned white by the screen. The sky is dirt grey, a drained blue low down, the stream afloat in the hooded dark of the trees. The grass glitters.

It was like this when.

When.

When what?

Something terrible happened on an afternoon just like this, but he cannot even begin to describe what, or even when that terrible thing was. He rests his hand on the left-hand side of his chest and scrunches the fine hair with his nails.

'This is the original file, your private repo.'

'Yes.'

Frank reads. An hour passes, more. The ping of rooks and then there they are, a loose cloud of black fragments, rising and falling over the stream. A jag of rainwater on the window shivers in the unfelt breeze. He removes his hand from his chest and splays his palm on the pane, to feel the cold of it, if he can – the realness of weather.

'I always thought... it reads like a sequel, to *Endless Love*. What you have so far.'

The story goes on. It stops. It goes on. It stops. It goes on. It stops.

'Are you okay, Andrew? You look a bit peaky.'

The humming is back, a very quiet sound, nearly indistinguishable from the white noise of the air. He lifts his toes as if it came from under the boards. Taps the lime plaster wall with his fist and tries to smile. But he knows where it comes from. The rooks ping and drift over the bare muscled slope.

'Do you hear that?'

'The birds?'

'The humming.'

Though he knows the visitor cannot hear it, because the humming is inside him, low down in the slim boat of his belly.

'I think we'd better go. I feel. I feel. I don't know.'

Frank takes his arm but the corridor is not quite wide enough for two. Andrew's left arm makes a soft hissing noise down the plain bulbous wall, knocks a tame pale picture of fishing boats askew. He tries to pull away from the wall and it is Frank now who hunches up and drags against the plaster. There is white dust in the folds of his dressing gown.

They make it downstairs, a controlled fall down the stairs – Frank strains to support his weight on the landing. His legs do not move properly, nor can he feel them. A bedroom would have been the sensible choice though he is no longer sure where the bedrooms are, what they look like. He remembers a large red bed in a hotel in Ghent, a boy's single bed in a black terraced house, a bed showroom where he bounced on the mattresses and his girlfriend giggled and refused to join him.

Random images of beds, associations. Her body pale in the long blue mirror somewhere; his body, slimmer, younger, legs crossed on the sunken mattress. A musty smell, and the smell of old cooking fat, from the B. & B. kitchen. They have only just met and it would be nice to know her name.

Andrew lies down on the sofa, props his too-long legs on the armrest. Frank asks his glasses to take a picture: his smile is lopsided, apologetic. Takes another and another. He will close his eyes for a moment and when he opens them again Frank will be gone. He tugs his dressing gown up over his torso but it falls away again. No matter. He is sure Frank has seen it all before. He shuts his eyes. That infernal humming. Nothing.

*

Frank watches Andrew from the easy chair, his hands knitted over one bobbing knee. A woman appears in the doorway, her straight hair a mix of raven black and dark grey. He starts to rise and she waves him down again. The visitor mouths *wow* and the woman – her mouth is red rust, her eyes a flat painted blue – nods her head vigorously. He looks over at the pictures on the mantel: the daughter, who lives here, who leads the Trust.

She kneels next to Andrew, pulls the dressing gown down a little more and fumbles at the side of his stomach. She flips back a small rectangular section of flesh, pink, veined beneath, like real skin, to reveal a small brass-coloured nozzle and a flashing red light.

'What did you think?'

'I think that may have been one of the most profound experiences of my life.'

'Ha. I'm glad. My father would smile at that. Vain old Daddy. He did like his fans.'

'Lovely man though.'

'Yes, lovely. Full of love.'

The woman pulls a small chrome suitcase up to her right knee. Extracts a coil of scratched transparent tubing and attaches it to the valve. The red light turns green and a black liquid jumps up the tube.

'I have to drain the coffee. There's another little box for the toast but I can take that out later.'

'Is the sofa original?'

'It's almost the only thing that isn't. It's specially built, a glorified giant charger, really. It probably needs a service; Andrew doesn't seem to last as long as he did these days.'

*

They drink herb tea in the kitchen, stare out at the dimming garden and the darkening hills. The house reproduces the writer's last day. When her mother got back from town he seemed to be sleeping and she let him be for an hour, perhaps more, before she realised. A doctor took the usual on-site MMR, but the pattern was already weak, breaking down; still it was enough to construct this replica, with a little boost from AI.

'Why this day though? You don't mind my asking? It must be difficult seeing your dad die every day. And you live here, don't you, behind the walls?'

'Andrew is not my dad.'

'No.'

'But yes. Yes at first. Not now… I'm used to it now. Why this day, why this day… because everything had been written, everything he would ever write. A week earlier and at least three of the chapters would be missing. He wrote fast, did Dad, when he wanted to. Plus, he was never one to evade mortality, the darker side.'

'And nor are you.'

'Death, even a false one, is a useful reminder to everyone who comes here that this isn't just a fairground show. That my dad was a human being as well as a great writer.'

'One of the last of the great writers.'

'Yes. One of the last.'

The daughter pushes the sway of hair away from her face, the gesture from the photo. She slides off the saloon stool and tips the remains of her tea into the sink; it is getting late, he has overstayed his welcome and she has work to do. He shows his palms, what he is about to do, then touches her shoulders and purses his lips at the air to either side of her face. Because she too is living history.

Frank can't resist a last look at Andrew on his sofa. His left hand hangs down – an authentic touch, he was told, though there will be nobody here to see it before he wakes – and his stomach is a low white pillow in the dark of the room. The battered paperback, an expense, replaced regularly, is posted beneath his raised legs. The writer looks asleep, alive. He finds himself pulling his shoes on, his coat, as quietly as he can, as if the action of his going might wake his hero.

Dead Friend's Coat

Kate Lockwood Jefford

On the first anniversary of my mother's untimely death, after waking with the words *corpse, corpus christi, corpuscle,* circling in the mists of my early morning mind, I found a letter on the doormat. A long narrow envelope. Brown. Handwritten in black ink. Upright capitals, uniform lower case. Tentative loops. Nothing flourished or fancy. The hand of a woman my mother's age. A woman taught to write in a post-war classroom, head bowed, and upper body bent over an A5 exercise book with blue and red lines spaced precisely to keep her prose in check. A second-class stamp – thrifty, also like my mother.

I boiled the kettle to steam the envelope open – a habit I've been unable to break since the years my mother lived with me – and slipped out a single sheet of paper folded twice. A scent of almonds and vanilla as two lines of the dense, typed block of text leapt out at me:

This is the saddest letter I have ever written.
and:
My beloved Eve is gone.

Eve. An image came to mind: a brushstroke sketch of a woman in shades of beige and butterscotch. A woman I'd known briefly two years earlier and not seen since. A woman my own age, dead. A first for me. An excited revving of my pulse.

My mother always said I was morbid.

I propped the letter against the telephone answering machine where – much to my satisfaction – it hid the red light flashing for the messages stacking up on the tape – the latest ignored calls from my particularly bitter ex and my ever-needy, petulant sisters.

*

It was the second of November. A day drab and damp enough to chill through flesh to bone. Expired Halloween lanterns leered from doorsteps and bin-side pyres. The clocks had just gone back. Many people were wearing black.

The patients in my morning clinic failed to engage my interest. I gave them their allotted times. Let them talk.

*

I'd met Eve in a draughty room above the Black Cat pub in deepest Hackney. An eight-week course of evening workshops for people wanting to develop an act for the growing alternative comedy circuit. It was 1991. I was trying to take my life in a different direction. The course was run by an emaciated, chain-smoking man who fancied himself as Lenny Bruce. He told us comedy was tough and none of us would get anywhere.

Eve didn't join in the bitching in the bar after workshops, or the banter, rough-cut with innuendo. She'd sit sipping Beaujolais bright as arterial blood, her smile glistening with lip balm.

We'd both lived south of the river and used to take the bus back together. Normally, I prefer to travel alone, but it was always too late, and I was too tired to fabricate an excuse. The first thing Eve told me about herself was that she had diabetes. 'Type I,' she said. People used to tell me things like that when they found out I was a doctor. I didn't like it.

Eve lived on the edge of Blackheath, just before the turn for the Blackwall Tunnel in a quiet, spacious flat painted in lemony pastels. A velvet sofa the colour of strawberry jam slouched long and low along one wall of the high-ceilinged lounge. It was like being inside a giant Victoria sandwich.

First time I went, I admired a camel-coloured woollen coat lined with faux leopardskin hanging from a hook in the hallway.

'Try it on,' she'd said.

It was vintage. 1950s. The sort of thing my mother wore when I was still an only child, when it was just the two of us before all my sisters were born. A caped collar, three-quarter sleeves, three mother-of-pearl buttons like discs of marble cake. I like old things. It fitted well.

'Have it,' she said.

On the way home I dug my hands into the large square pockets. A packet of Dextrose Energy tablets on one side. Half a Twix on the other. I used to take Dextrose to feed my brain when I got up at 4am to study for A levels in the hushed tick-tock of the kitchen clock before my sisters got up and started making all their noise.

I ate the Twix.

*

I wrote back to Eve's mother:

> I am shocked to hear about Eve. She was such a nice and generous person.
> Sincere condolences.

I also mentioned the coat and suggested we could meet if she'd like to. I carried the letter in my bag almost a week before posting it, after which I regretted the bit about the coat and meeting up. Then I didn't hear back from her straight away, which irritated me.

There was a letter from the Royal College of Psychiatrists informing me I'd passed their qualifying exam, and several communications from the solicitor regarding my mother's ongoing probate. After the divorce my mother had reverted to her maiden name, the same as that of a serial killer who made the front page of all the papers one hot sticky August in the late sixties. It turned out my mother wasn't a stranger to violence either.

*

We used to rehearse at Eve's. My place was floor-to-ceiling boxes of my mother's stuff, and the phone rang at all hours due to time differences – my sisters – or alcohol – the ex. And anyway, I've never enjoyed or encouraged visitors. Her act – which she described as a 'skit' – consisted of comic covers of sixties' pop songs. She backcombed and lacquered her honey-blonde hair and wore a candyfloss-pink suede miniskirt. I loaned her a pair of knee-high black patent leather zip-up boots. She still looked like a child playing dressing up. I could barely watch, but audiences liked her in the same way everyone gushed over my sisters when they sang their stupid songs. Did their stupid dances.

When she returned the boots the inner lining around the heel and toes was torn and stained with old, brown dried blood.

My act was a commentary on mother-daughter relationships. Some people thought I went too far in using my sisters' actual names, but I wanted something edgy, sharp. Subtle and sophisticated, not belly laughs. Eve shrieked and howled in every pause as if it was a cue for canned laughter. It made me want to slap her.

Eve's mother came to the showcase at the end of the course. A tall narrow woman wearing tight-fitting herringbone tweeds in shades of rust and grey. Brown hair on the turn. Black leather lace-up flats. I recalled the stage lights reflected in her glasses, setting her eyes ablaze like yellow fires. A werewolf in winged spectacles. I wondered what she'd made of it all.

*

Finally, one Saturday morning, another long brown envelope addressed in black ink landed, flat and alone, on the doormat.

> I would very much like to meet you. I sometimes have to work near Holborn. I do not know how you are situated, but if you're in that vicinity, we could meet for coffee?

*

I pulled Eve's coat from where I'd wedged it between two of my mother's bouclé jackets in the wardrobe. The wool was scratchy like old blankets, the faux leopardskin lining smooth and cool as sand on a beach at dusk. A row of short, thick, parallel marks on the top half of the left sleeve, as if from a grubby-fingered grip, most likely from when the bitter ex last escorted me off his premises. It smelled of stale biscuits, raisins, a hint of soy sauce. I hung it near an open window. It rotated slowly one way, then the other, like a little girl doing a coy twirl.

*

The café near Holborn was long and narrow with Formica table-tops and melamine ashtrays. Mirrors along both walls made it seem busier and louder. Eve's mother – recognisable from the tweeds and winged spectacles – was sitting at a table facing the door. She stood to shake my hand – a cold bony squeeze of my fingers that made me flinch. Her skin was thin with a translucent sheen, almost see-through, as if the course of her grief had sluiced her out. On the seat next to her was a bulky brown leather handbag, exactly like one my mother had. I knew my way around that bag, its cavities, pockets and zipped compartments: where to find her keys, her purse (for the change and frazzled fivers I thought she wouldn't miss), the balled-up mesh shopping bag, emery boards, tweezers, tissues. The loose boiled sweets coated in crumbs and nail dust rolling around at the bottom.

After the business of ordering – Earl Grey for her, black coffee for me – I repeated that I was shocked to hear about Eve.

Eve's mother dropped her gaze to examine her tea. 'I no longer wonder what more I could have done,' she said. 'I don't blame myself. You shouldn't either.'

That sort of guilt hadn't occurred to me. Eve hadn't looked after herself – I'd seen the expired vials of insulin in the butter compartment above the wine and chocolate in her fridge.

'I would have liked more contact with Eve's consultant,' her mother continued, 'I had information that would have helped her in Eve's case. Information Eve wouldn't have shared. But she didn't approach me. Not once.' She paused, looked up, straight at me, 'Doctors can be terribly unforthcoming, don't you think?'

I didn't want to get into any of that. I lifted Eve's coat out of the large Marks and Spencer's carrier bag I'd brought it in. Her mother reached to pull it to her face and inhaled deeply: first the collar, then the lining, sleeves, and underarms.

'Put it on, would you?' she said.

I stepped into the aisle and slipped my arms into the sleeves. Eve's mother directed me to turn one way and the other, inspecting me. As if considering a purchase.

'It's such a good fit. You're the exact same size as my Eve,' she said. 'You go in and out in the exact same places. It's just the hair that's different.'

I said it was generous of Eve to give me the coat. I sounded trite. Eve's mother told me she knew Eve had liked me. She said to keep the coat. To wear it next time we met.

'I want to hold on to Eve's flat,' she said, when we parted at Holborn tube, 'for sentimental reasons, you understand. I was very fortunate in letting it to a kind and caring gentleman.'

*

Returning on the train, I thought about Eve's mother's skinny arms and pinchy fingers, so unsuited for holding or comfort. And I wondered about the cushioned surfaces in Eve's flat, the soft, spongy furnishings and thick pile carpets. A gentler landing. A lesser knock to the head. I pictured a kind and caring gentleman sitting on her sofa, and I wondered if he could smell strawberry jam and butter cream. Taste it on his tongue.

Back home I slotted Eve's coat into its place between the bouclé jackets. Now and again I put it on. It really was a good fit. I wore it. The weather was still cold enough.

*

The next meeting in the Holborn café, Eve's mother was sitting in the same place facing the same way. Watching the door. This time it reminded me of my paranoid patients. I sensed a ripple in the air around her – she appeared twitchy, excited. When she saw me in the coat she plunged a bony arm elbow-deep into the brown leather handbag and produced a paper bag from which she pulled a wig. Honey-blonde. I paused, felt a thrill shudder my shoulders. Goosepimple my arms.

'It's real hair,' she said. 'Try it on.'

I turned it over to reveal the tight mesh of synthetic filaments the human hair was knotted onto, then flipped it back and onto my head. Eve's mother leaned across to tuck stray strands behind my ears, finger the fringe this way and that, before sitting back to assess her work, lick her thumb and move in again to flick the tip of my nose.

'A lash,' she said.

Up close her smell of carbolic soap recalled a scene from childhood. My mother in waist-clinching white knickers strip-washing at the sink in a stone-cold bathroom. On the wall above her, a single-bar electric heater operated by a pull-cord. Rarely used because of always, always saving electricity. My mother's sloping shoulders, the fleshy corrugations of her sides, the flap and flip of the flannel on her damp, pinkened skin, scooping into armpits, swiping beneath breasts lifted one at a time. Bunions jutting from chilblained feet placed on the doubled-over towel to catch drips. Afterwards, covering every surface, a fine layer of talcum powder like a private indoor dusting of virgin snow.

Eve's mother looked dagger-straight at me – searching, intense. I looked sideways in the mirror. At her and me. A woman my mother's age and a woman my age with honey-blonde hair instead of red. The wig felt tight, itchy all over, like the berets my mother used to crochet from unravelled jumper wool and make me wear all winter.

I turned to face Eve's mother and opened my mouth, but she raised a hand to halt me. 'Ssshh,' she said, 'no need to speak. Let's just be, shall we? People talk too much, don't you think? Talk, talk, talk. Yet never act.'

And so we sat in our bubble of silence inside the chat and clatter bouncing off surfaces of Formica and glass. Outside, the drone of double-decker buses up and down Kingsway, the rumble of the Central Line dungeon-deep below.

'I'm so glad we've met,' she said. 'It means so much. You were a good and true friend to Eve. I know I'm not wrong.'

*

Days later, the postman rang the bell and handed over an armful of brown paper packaging. First class and tracked. I had to sign.

There was so much string and Sellotape, I took the kitchen scissors to it. Inside the package, wrapped in fine white tissue paper like a high-end boutique, were several parcels in various sizes, bulky and soft, yet firm when prodded. Like stuffed toys, the flesh of an upper arm. The smell of mothballs, lavender and washing powder, as I opened them, one at a time. Two size 10 polyester pencil skirts: one cream, the other custard yellow. A short-sleeved crew-necked jumper in chocolate brown cashmere, 34-inch chest. A peach silk petticoat edged in red velvet with matching bra and knickers, size S. A pair of black diamond-patterned nylon tights, shoe-size 4 to 7.

Everything fitted. I could have been shoehorned into Eve's body, and she into mine.

I started to wear Eve's clothes and wig around the house,

initially for an hour now and then. Gradually for longer periods. And more often. At first, I was restrained. Hell, it's just clothes, a hairpiece, I thought, not necromancy. So I stopped resisting.

Sometimes you have to act.

*

Making dinner one evening I got thick, red oily splashes of pomodoro sauce on Eve's cashmere jumper and sponged them off with the corner of a dishcloth. Would Eve do the same, I wondered, or leave them? Maybe not even notice?

I thought about a weekend masterclass in method acting I'd attended once, back when I was still trying to realign my life. We were instructed to choose someone we knew well and list their likes, dislikes, their taste in food, films, books, clothes, their manners, and attitudes, what they thought about others, what others made of them, and so on. I'd used one of my sisters even though I was sick to death of them. I didn't want to use my ex, and it would have been impossible to use my mother. 'Homework' was to spend Saturday evening as this person – to adopt their style of clothing, body posture, facial expression, tone of voice and mannerisms, as well as their habits and behaviours: to eat the food they liked, watch their preferred TV shows, read their choice in books etc.

And I thought about how little I knew about Eve – her childhood, where she went to school, if she went to university, what work she did, or even why she'd enrolled on the comedy course. Her surname was the same as a wartime spy my mother had been fascinated by. I don't recall her ever mentioning a father. It was all a blank. I'd never asked, and she never said.

I could imagine my mother thinking Eve 'nice', praising

her generosity in a *Why can't you be more like Eve?* way. To me, Eve was someone who'd suffered many knockbacks. Disappointments. She'd never voiced this, but it lurked in the unasked, the unsaid, the gaps around her. The bruises on her arms and legs. Her cracked and thirsty lips. The pear-drop tang of ketones on her breath.

Being in Eve's company had exhausted me, as if she was sucking the energy out of me, the way my sisters sucked my mother dry. And I thought about my mother's precipitous departure from our lives, and my sisters, scatter-gunned around the globe. Their scatter, her gun.

I began to dream about Eve. To taste her – sugary, with a tang of antiseptic – in my morning tea, my food, my wine. Smell her in the sheets on my bed, on my skin, my hair, the dry air of my office. Her mother always lurked in these dreams too – in the form of various women, but always in winged spectacles and smelling of carbolic soap.

One night my ex called round – something he still did occasionally, to lay a fresh grievance at my feet – and Eve answered. Confusion and panic tugged his face at odd angles.

'She doesn't live here anymore,' I said, my smile glistening with lip balm. 'She moved. I don't know exactly where to.'

The perplexity hardening into fear in his eyes was very pleasing.

*

Eve's mother telephoned to arrange the next meeting in the café in Holborn. I didn't remember giving her my number.

She was already seated with her cup of Earl Grey, a black coffee for me in the opposite place, and began speaking before I'd had a chance to remove Eve's coat, so I kept it on. 'The kind and caring gentleman has become reconciled with his wife,' she said. 'Men aren't good on their own. Not like us.'

She paused to lift the cup of Earl Grey to her thin pale lips and take a sip before replacing it on its saucer. It was then that I noticed the keys – one brass, one silver – lying side by side on the pale blue Formica, looped together through a single ring.

'Consequently, I'm looking for a new tenant for Eve's property,' she continued, shooting me a quick glance, checking my reaction. 'I've heard a doctor may be interested. A woman doctor. What do you think?'

I removed Eve's coat – which had begun to itch like hell – and folded it on the seat next to me.

'What size is she?' I said, reaching for my coffee, suddenly parched.

Politics

Jonathan Edwards

When I was a child, my uncle lived in a series of extraordinary houses. He was a vicar and, with each new posting, each new parish, came a home even more elaborate than the last.

There was the huge, twin-staircased place, where you could run downstairs and look down the hall to see your cousins, standing at the foot of the other staircase, waving at you out of the distance. The place was so enormous and rambling, that when you played hide and seek it could take hours to be found. Hiding under the bed or inside a cupboard in a creaking bedroom, you'd get scared that everyone in the house had been murdered by a headless horseman or else gone down the pub. Then you'd step from the room to call your cousin's name, and discover that you'd lost the game now and there were still three more people to find.

There was the upside-down house on top of a hill, which had a cousin's bedroom right next to the front door and the coat-stand, and a living room upstairs, with a big window looking out over the town. You could nip downstairs to the toilet or to bed, only to find yourself, running upstairs to watch TV or make an out-of-breath sandwich in the gravity-defying kitchen. You could spend an hour looking out of the big window that was better than a TV, at the streets you'd walked through and the corners you'd lurked on, pointing and looking closely to check if you were still there. Going to sleep in my conventional terraced, I'd think of my cousins, dreaming their ground-floor dreams.

Then there was the place slap-bang next to the churchyard, which somehow also had a putting green at the end of the drive. Playing draughts or toy cars with your cousins, you could look out the window, past the dresses and vestments blowing on the line, read the inscription on the tombstone of someone who'd been dead for forty years. Then you could walk down the long drive, take a sharp left and find yourself hiring a putter from the man in the little booth. You could spend an hour keeping an eye out that your uncle didn't fiddle his score with the little pencil they'd lent you, as you lined up shots and imagined yourself standing on a fairway in the Highlands, in a Fair Isle jumper and emerald visor.

In all of these houses lived my cousin Hywel. He had two sisters too, remote figures who sometimes played with us and were sometimes busy doing something unclear. But it was Hywel I loved. I loved him in the way that only an only child, with a cousin who's seven years older than him, taller and more knowledgeable about football and music, can love someone. When I was struggling to break into the school football team, and would spend a match on the sidelines in the football boots I'd had for Christmas, waiting for my teacher to call me onto the pitch, kicking bits of mud at a goal in my mind, I would think of Hywel. I'd imagine him giving me secret coaching sessions in the garden of his house, passing on all his tricks and tips, so at one of the PE afternoons I could go on a mazy dribble, beat my whole class, have the teacher falling on his bum, and score.

Or when the bigger boys, who terrorised the back lane behind our house on BMXs, chased me from one end of it to the other and called me names I didn't understand, I'd imagine Hywel. He'd just be standing there in the lane, his hands on his hips, and all the kids would be coming up to me, one after the other, apologising and offering me a go on their bikes.

Hywel, though, did not love me back. I knew this for many reasons. There was the time when we spent the hours of my visit to his house sorting through his toy cars on his bedroom floor. He said he was too old for them now, but they might just suit someone like me, and I could pick whichever ones I liked. I spent hours driving them all round the Brands Hatch of his carpet, agonising over which ones to keep. But when my parents called for me to go and I was gathering my picks together, overjoyed to have something of Hywel's, he said, 'Leave them there, Owen. I've changed my mind.'

Then there was the time he told his mum he'd take me to karate with him – 'Don't worry, I'll look after him.' Walking along with his friends through a Cwmbran evening as traffic zoomed past, I felt as old as they were, as they talked about punches and flying kicks and third dans. Their teacher, Hywel said, knew how to kill a man with just a movement of his hand, but he'd only pass on the knowledge if you went to enough lessons. When we got to the leisure centre and Hywel and his friends changed into their karate kits, I asked him what I should wear, but he turned away then. Through the door of the hall, I watched as he and his friends knelt and bowed to a pudgy man sitting cross-legged at the front. Then Steve, one of his friends, with a bandage round his hand which wasn't big enough to sign, a sprained wrist which stopped him doing karate, walked me home. I asked him if he'd hurt himself in a fist fight down an alley. 'Nah, butt,' he said. 'Fell over in the play yard.'

When Hywel came to visit, it was agony. I'd plan and plan for ages, line up all my favourite games for us to play and treasured toys to show him, think of things I could ask him and secrets I could tell. His parents would invariably show up hours late because of some emergency with a parishioner. Often when the door opened they'd be standing there with one of Hywel's sisters, and Hywel himself would be at home swotting or else off down the pub. If he was there, he'd spend his time hanging round the vol-au-vents my mother had spent the afternoon making, and asking her if she had any more beer. I looked down at all my treasures and knew there was absolutely nothing here, that I had absolutely nothing to tempt him.

*

When my father opened the front door, there was a man dressed like a baked bean standing there.

It was 1992, and I was eleven, and Wales were going to win the General Election. Wales was a bald man on a beach on the telly with a suit on, hand in hand with his wife, falling over in the waves, then getting up and punching the air. He talked like us but louder, and pointed at people, and my mother loved him. Sometimes posh people sat behind desks on the TV and made fun of his accent, and my mother shouted at them, and my nan hissed.

Meanwhile, my father spent all his time rebuilding a bright orange MG Roadster in the garage. I'd go out to call him in for tea and find two overalled legs sticking out from under a sweeping orange bonnet. Rebuilding a car looked a lot to me like breaking it. I tried many times to tell him a car wouldn't go if he replaced its wheels with bricks like that, but he wouldn't listen. Sometimes I'd spend all Saturday afternoon out in the garage, handing him spanners and talking to his feet, to the rhythm of an unscrewing nut. My father was a voice coming from somewhere I couldn't see. I'd ask him if he thought Hywel might come over next week or if Hywel might want to know I'd started the last game for the school first eleven. I asked if we could rearrange our house so that I could sleep upside-down like Hywel did, and then we could go and visit him in the upside-down house and tell him all about it.

I kept forgetting that Hywel wasn't there though, because he was away in university, studying Politics. In a vague way, this connected him in my mind with the bald man on the telly and with Wales winning the General Election, and I thought that perhaps Hywel was working with the bald man somehow and that was why Wales were suddenly doing so well.

Now my father had finished his bright orange car and it was sitting outside the front of our house, shining, and a man dressed like a baked bean was standing at the door.

The man dressed like a baked bean announced himself as Emperor Bean of the Imperial Bean Party, and he gave my father a leaflet. He said he was in the area looking for votes, and had spotted the fabulously shiny bright orange car. The bean costume was an all-over orange bodystocking, and he also had on an orange cape, and an orange mask which made him look like a superhero and meant you could only see his eyes, moving about. He had orange trainers on too, and when I looked I could see they were a pair of battered Dunlop Green Flash like Hywel wore, which he'd painted orange and mostly made a good job of but missed a bit here and there. His leaflet said, 'Vote for Beans!'

What Emperor Bean wanted, as well as our vote, was a photograph of himself next to the bright orange car, which he would add to his leaflets and ask the local paper to run. For publicity purposes, he said, he would call the car the Beanmobile. Perhaps there could even be a photo of him behind the wheel, and perhaps he could even offer my father some money to drive him around during the election, while he made announcements about the Imperial Bean Party through a bullhorn.

My father laughed. He'd been working on the car for six months, and it had been out front for two weeks and no one had paid it a blind bit of attention, and my mother and my nan were driving him crazy going on and on about the Labour Party and the election all the time. So he grabbed his camera and went outside, and I followed.

A few shots of Emperor Bean standing in front of the car, his cape billowing, and then I asked my father if I could be in the photo. I had a vague sense that involving myself in all this could impress Hywel. We were standing there in front of the car, looking into the camera my father was holding, me and Emperor Bean, striking poses like we were limbering up for a fight, when my mother and my nan came walking down the street.

My father let the camera dangle round his neck, and turned to my mother. 'This is Emperor Bean,' he said.

*

In the next few weeks, in the run-up to the election, I drove my mother crazy talking about Emperor Bean. Our house was on the main road to a polling station, and I had tried to stick the Emperor's 'Vote for Beans!' leaflet to our living room window, to influence the electorate and generate a last-minute swing vote. My mother, though, was even more house-proud than she was loyal to Labour, and there was no way she was having Blu-Tack or Bean propaganda staining her windows. We debated the issue thoroughly around the breakfast table.

'This is freedom of speech,' I said to her.

'And this is my living room window,' she said.

'I want to impress Hywel,' I said. 'I want to swing the election!'

'The best I can offer, Owen,' she said, 'is that you put the leaflets in your bedroom window. No Blu-Tack though. You'll have to prop them there.'

'But no one will look up there,' I said.

'I'd take what I can get if I were you,' said my father, from behind the paper.

'If my bedroom was downstairs like Hywel's,' I said, 'I'd be able to have a lot more impact.'

'For the last and final time,' said my mother, 'we're not turning the bloody house upside bloody down. It's your bedroom window or nothing.'

My mother had kept on and on at my father about the photograph of Emperor Bean in front of the orange MG, said she'd never be able to show her face in the street again if the photo was in the paper. In the end, the paper hadn't used it – Emperor Bean told my father they'd promised they would, but something must have gone wrong. Things often went wrong, he said, and he was often grappling with a biased media. My father did show the photo of me and Emperor Bean standing next to the orange MG to my uncle though, and they both laughed heartily, and my uncle said later he'd told Hywel all about it, and Hywel thought it was great.

I propped the photo and the Bean leaflets in my bedroom window, and waited for election day. I had my plan all ready. I was going to spend the day banging the window and waving at people passing below and get them to look up.

*

One of the best things about election day was that the school was a polling station, which meant you got a day off. In the morning I spent some time in my bedroom window, waving at people below, banging the window and trying to get them to look up. Most people didn't hear me, and one or two looked round, puzzled as to where the banging was coming from, then walked on. Big Jim from down the street looked up, saw me and waved back, thinking I was just saying hello or playing a game. Some people squinted a bit but couldn't read the leaflets, and some I heard saying to each other 'What the hell's all that about beans?' and 'Do you think that boy's okay up there?' Finally, old Mrs Godfrey from next door came round to tell my mother she was trying to get some ironing done and all she could hear was *bang bang bang* all the bloody morning, and my mother shouted up the stairs to me, and that was my campaigning days over. I wasn't a bit surprised to be honest. The Godfreys had always been Labour.

In the afternoon, a bunch of us from the street went out for a bike ride with our mothers. The plan was to go to the Sirhowy Valley Walk, the nature area on the way out of the village, but our mothers were always a bit rubbish with directions, and after a fair bit of pushing our bikes uphill, with them walking behind us, we found ourselves on an industrial site, factories and skips and Portakabins all around us. We could see down below and off to the right the beautiful Sirhowy Valley Walk, folks whizzing in and out between trees on their bikes, or strolling along laughing, or roller-skating backwards past the squirrels.

The only thing between us and there was the long steep downhill from the factory. That was very welcome given the steep bike-pushing walk uphill, and me and the other kids jumped on our bikes and started accelerating downhill, as our mothers walked behind us.

My parents had always been the type that, looking back, I can see now as overprotective. Or perhaps even as appropriately protective, given some of the stuff the world does. I'd be out with my friends playing football, when they'd drive up in the car to the playing fields, my mother in the passenger seat looking worried. Then they'd whisk me home, my friends laughing at me and switching up the teams to accommodate my absence. Or I'd come home and say that my friends were planning a trip to Newport at half-term to spend their money on computer games, and my mother would say to write down the ones I wanted and she'd be sure to get my dad to pick them up for me when he was in town.

If I'd been thinking about all that, I may have been able to put what happened next into context, might have known how best to respond to my mother's shouted words. But, as we hurtled down that road at increasing speed, and the other mothers just ambled along, listening to the birds or chatting I guess, I heard my own mother calling from behind me. 'Owen!' she was calling. 'Owen! Stop!'

In a second I had slammed my brakes on and, of course, was flying over the handlebars. I landed partly on my tooth and partly on my chin, which ensured that part of my tooth was lost, is probably still sitting on that industrial estate now, all these years later. It also ensured that, by the time my mother got to me, picked me up and held me against her, blood was flowing and flowing from my chin.

I'd only ever previously known my mother to run on School Sports Day, when she tucked her skirt into her knickers, kicked off her shoes and beat all the other mothers, including several in tracksuits and Lycra, in the egg and spoon race. Now she ran again, holding my bleeding chin tight against her dress. I watched the world rushing by through teary eyes, heard her breathing, her heart banging, tight against my ear. The older boys cycled ahead of us to carry the disastrous news through the village and, before I knew it, my father was drawing up alongside us in the bright orange MG. I spotted the flyers for the Imperial Bean Party in the back, next to a bullhorn, though he'd sworn to my mother and my nan he'd have nothing to do with canvassing.

'Let's have a look, then,' he said, touching my arm and, when I turned to show him my chin, he said, 'Bloody hell, boy.' Then, seeing me look away, he said, 'Don't worry, champ, you'll have a cracking-looking scar there. Chicks'll dig you. You'll be able to show Hywel.'

My mother, though, was scowling at him, holding some tissues from her handbag against my chin. 'Geraint,' she said. 'Hospital.'

My father turned the key and the bright orange car drove off.

*

The main thing about the hospital was waiting. There was waiting for X-rays, waiting for nurses, waiting for doctors. There was waiting to go into another room and do more waiting. After the initial treatments, when the uniformed folks could see what they were dealing with, when they knew what problems I was presenting them with, there was more and more waiting, as the danger was over now, the bleeding had been stopped, and it was a case of waiting for the checks, the double checks, the say-so.

There was the bit where they put the big injection into my chin – the worst bit, by a country mile – so I wouldn't feel anything, then sewed my chin up with a long bit of string, like it was a torn rug. There was the bit where they gave me an X-ray and showed me a picture of my jaw, the inside of me hanging on the wall there like an artwork. Somewhere between it all, my father said that he'd rung my uncle to let him know.

That did it, of course. From then on, all I could think about was whether Hywel would show up, to check I was okay. I could tell him about my election campaigning of course, my recent brushes with the world of politics, but really even all that paled into insignificance in light of my near-death experience on an industrial estate. He was bound to be impressed by that, bound to mention my bravery, my maturity, the stitches in my chin, the gap in my teeth, bound to think me worthy now of toy cars and karate. Perhaps he'd even have one of his favourite cars in his pocket to give me.

So through all the waiting in waiting rooms, all the sitting on couches, all the *Brave boy*s and half-drawn curtains, I waited, not for treatment, but for Hywel to be there. I asked and asked my father what my uncle had said, asked for his words *exactly*, though I didn't dare ask if Hywel was coming. I only knew that he would.

Soon, though, the last doctor said we could go, there was no need for an overnight, just go to the doctor in a week to have the stitches out. Avoid contact sports and running round too much, be careful in the bathtub. I sat there, my legs dangling over the edge of the bed I was sitting on, and imagined all the excuses my mother would have now to keep me in the house. It was worse than that, though. We were about to go home, and Hywel hadn't come.

It was then, though, as we were gathering everything to go, when I heard a pair of feet coming down the corridor, heard them approaching, getting nearer, heard them stop outside the curtain round my bed. This was it. I looked under the curtain, and saw the trainers there. I saw that they were orange.

'Excuse me,' said a voice, 'is that Mr Jenkins?'

My father opened the curtain, and there was Emperor Bean of the Imperial Bean Party. He had his mask off, and underneath was the face of a balding, clean-shaven fellow, with chubby jowls which made him look no less like a bean, in all honesty, than he did with his mask on. His cape was ripped, his bodystocking torn in several places, and his flabby gut was poking through the holes.

'Huw!' said my father. 'What the bloody Christ happened to you?'

'Ah, you know,' said Emperor Bean, 'that twat from the Crazy Pink Bubble-Mongeese Party. I started winding him up about the real plural being mongooses, not mon*geese*, and he just went for me. Politics, Geraint. Nasty business.'

'It *is* mongooses, though,' said my mother.

'I know it is, Mrs Jenkins,' said the Emperor, looking disconsolate, 'I know it only too well. But sometimes there's a line you simply do not cross.'

'You all right, Huw?' said my dad.

'Yeah, fine,' he said. 'Shaken up a bit, butt. Main injury to the bodystocking. They're just running some tests. Never mind about me, though. They told me at the polling station what happened, and I wanted to come down and see the young fella. My co-star from the photo! How you doing, young man?'

'I'm okay,' I said.

'Course you are,' he said. 'Tough guy like you. Do you know, I think I got more votes than ever this time, because of that photo. Everyone talks about it. The little guy posing like a boxer. We could do it even better now, with that scar you're going to have.'

'The next election!' I said. My mother rolled her eyes.

'I wanted to bring you this,' said Emperor Bean, holding out his hand.

It was a Dinky toy version of an MG Roadster. It had been silver underneath but the Emperor had painted it in orange and, although you could see the silver paint coming through, he hadn't done too bad a job.

'I was going to use these as a promo for the next campaign,' he said. 'This is a prototype. But I wanted to give it to you.'

'Going to?' said my father.

'Yeah, Geraint,' said the Emperor, 'I'm done with politics. It's all over. This mongoose shit has sent me right over the edge. Don't think I'm not grateful. It's been brilliant, what you've done for this campaign. My favourite campaign yet.'

'It's been good fun, Huw,' said my dad.

'I've given it a good few years,' said the Emperor, 'but it's time now. The missis is on at me anyway. Time for me to become a career man. It's time I really took I.T. seriously.'

'How did the election go?' said my mother.

'They'll be counting soon,' said the Emperor. 'Sure I'll lose my deposit again. The early talk is Conservatives by a landslide.'

'Shitting Jesus,' said my mother. 'Not again. Surely.'

Then someone outside in the corridor shouted 'Emperor? Huw Emperor, please.'

'Okay,' said the Emperor to me, 'just wanted to check in and see you were okay, little man. Stay strong! Stay orange! And see you soon.'

Then he turned, his ripped cape swishing, and he was gone.

*

I've still got that photo of me with the Emperor Bean, hanging on the wall in the kitchen, next to all the family pictures. It was the one and only family entry into politics really, though Hywel's carved out a decent career in the Civil Service since then. Last year, when his son was born, he made me his godfather. I've still got the scar on my chin too, still got the memories of how bloody painful it was, having the stitches out. My father must have been through umpteen different car rebuilds since then, and wherever that MG Roadster is now, I feel sure it isn't orange any more.

When I think about that whole time, about coming off my bike, about that election, I don't think about any of that, though. We found out next day that the bald man who was Wales had lost the election, and my mother said 'Shitting Jesus' again, and she still talks about it now, how things would have been completely different.

When I think of it all now, what I think about is coming home late that night, my chin different, and the house different, too, now that I was a boy with part of my tooth on a nearby industrial estate. I went straight upstairs to my room and, before my mother came up to tuck me in, I didn't think once about how my bedroom that could be downstairs was upstairs, how the living room could be the bathroom if things were only different, and how I could pop into my parents' bedroom to make a late-night sandwich or to boil the kettle.

I took the little orange car out of my pocket and I put it on the windowsill, in the place where no one but me would see it. It was caught in the beam from the street light outside, the little bits of silver coming through. And I looked around then at my things, my books, the posters on the wall, under the light of my A-Team lampshade. It was all where it belonged, one storey up in the world and all of it, all of it, was glowing with my survival.

Swim

Miranda Davies

She could taste salt in her mouth and the current tangled her legs. On the edge of her vision, cream and white houses swept the edge of the bay. This far out you couldn't smell the fried fish nor the eggy smoke from the hotel chimneys. Just rotting seaweed and sometimes a little petrol in the water.

'Dir ist nicht zu kalt?' he called. You're not too cold?

'No!' she answered him in English.

'You look pale,' he said, moving into the same language as her.

'That's how I always look,' she shouted back.

She could feel the cold creeping, tracing its fingers inside her bathing suit, up from the thighs, grabbing at her stomach, pinching her chest. Her sense of her own toes was vanishing into the water. She splashed her arms on the surface and kicked her legs. If I go in now, I'll die, she thought. If I go in now, everything will break.

'When did you learn swimming?' her father asked.

'Passover. Easter. The holiday I was eight. Mr Ramsey took me in and Mother watched.'

'Mr Ramsey?' her father asked, swimming closer.

'He had the farm next door to us. He had a big yellow beard and shot rabbits. His daughter was above me in school. Manon.'

It was tiring to talk.

'Manon.' Her father repeated the name. 'Like French. Will you swim with me? To the pier? It doesn't have to be a race.'

They turned their bodies in the water and started off, Anna lagging behind because she was curious to see how her father swam. He'd been behind her on the shore, getting in. She'd heard his labouring breath. Had not imagined that he had the energy nor youth to swim like her. His pale shoulders bobbed beneath the waves. He became sleek somehow.

She kicked furiously to catch him up, then dropped behind again, watching his grey-haired head dip below the surface. Her father's hands met each other. His body straightened. The further he went, the more he acquired a kind of grace. Anna pulled at the water with her hand, savouring the salt taste in her mouth, the quickening of blood in her limbs.

At the pier he reached up with one hand to steady himself and turned. She waved to him from a distance. The smile he gave her surprised her with its warmth.

'You let me win!' he called.

'My arms got tired.'

'Liar!'

She trod water for a minute and watched her father watching her. She thought she found him easier from a distance. She saw his brow furrow so she dug her arms into the water and set off.

'It was not good of me,' he told her as she swam closer. 'Good fathers let daughters win.'

'Do they?'

She was surprised by this. Perhaps it was true. Perhaps if he had been a better father he would have let her win. She had little sense of fathers, good or bad. Mr Ramsey, of course, he was a father. But most of the fathers had been gone, for years. You learned not to talk about them. Not to upset yourself. No one knew when anyone was coming home.

He swam towards her. 'Don't think too much. It was just a thing to say. Are you ready for chips?'

'No. Not yet. Can we stay out here?'

'Forever?'

Anna stroked the sea. She allowed her body to dance in its movement. She felt grown up out here; long-limbed, female. 'If we stay out, we could be anywhere. And if we're anywhere…' She couldn't finish the thought.

'International waters,' he said.

'Are we?' she asked. 'Here?'

Her father laughed. 'No. But if you swim far enough. And turn left at Ireland…'

'You're making fun,' she said.

'I'm not!' he told her, a little exasperated, slipping back into a more familiar tongue. 'I love it too. I've missed it. Though in the old place it was lakes. Never the sea. You looked across and there was always another side. Same country, just carrying on. I never swam anywhere where you could just keep going. Out and out. Until you struck whales and dolphins and mermaids.

'In Hutchinson we could see the sea, but not to swim in. Only to know that it was there. That it was hard to leave. There was a wire fence, but in summer we would sit on the grass sometimes and watch the colours of the sky on the surface of the water. The clouds and the way the sun came through at the edges and shot down beams like it was a painting from an Italian church.

'They brought us fish, the kitchens stank of fish. Kippers were the best thing. I learned that. With butter sometimes. Fried. Chicken eggs. Pepper. Yom Kippur!' Her father laughed. 'Yom kippers! That was the joke. A bit Manx. A bit German. A bit Jewish.'

Anna, still feeling stung, looked away to the shore, the

passing cyclists swooping silently along the promenade, holding their skirts down against the wind.

'Will we go in?' he asked.

There was anger in her mouth, stifling and hot.

'Will we burn the town and start again?' he asked her in English.

'Burn everything,' she told him. 'Not the people. Just the houses. Burn it all. Gone.'

Her father thought about this. 'Maybe that is what we are doing.'

She felt her face tense, her nose and lips quivering. 'You think we're burning it all down?'

The look he gave her had a touch of fear. 'Starting again?' he ventured.

She swam away from him, towards the shore. Her throat tight.

'Anna!'

She touched her cheek to the water.

'Anna?'

She could see her mother waiting on the stones.

'Anna!'

She found the bottom, feet slipping on the tumbling stones. Clattered to her knees, beneath the level of the waves for a moment, then let the force of the water carry her in. Her mother unfolded a towel.

By the time her father was out of the sea, her mother had gone up the stones for tea. His knitted bathers hung about the tops of his thighs. She could see the shape of his sex. The sag of his chest. His squinting gaze. She buried her head inside the towel.

She heard the rattle of stones as he approached. The catch of his breathing as he sat. She could imagine the folds of his belly and was repelled by them. What strange intimacy did these old people share with her?

Under the towel, music was playing. Lizbeth Webb was singing about the sun and the wine. Anna slipped into another world.

Her mother returned with two cups of milky tea. Sugar for Anna, or something like it. Not sweet enough for the real thing, and a tang of something bitter.

They sat in silence and listened to the children running behind them, the wind slapping the ropes against the flagpoles. Anna licked below the surface of the tea and scalded her tongue.

'Does Anna want an ice cream?' her father asked. Anna shrugged. But she let the towel fall off her shoulders and accepted the cardigan her mother handed her. They walked up to the promenade together. Anna held out the cup of sour, sweet liquid. Her father took it and drank a little down.

They climbed the stone steps and leant against the railings, facing out into the wind.

'You're very fierce,' her father said. He'd given up on English again.

'No,' she told him, 'I'm not fierce.'

'You're fiercer because you don't know how fierce you are.'

'I was just a bit sad. You can't go blowing these things up.'

'You don't know how much we fear you,' he told her.

She looked at him. He did not meet her eye.

'What does that mean?' she asked. 'I'm just a child.'

He snorted as he drank her tea. 'You've started to judge us,' he told her. 'It's only just beginning.'

'I'm asking questions. I'm trying to understand... you make me sound like a monster.'

Her father blew fiercely into the cup. 'You are a monster. Our monster.'

'I'm not a little girl. I don't feel little any more.'

'Did you get old, Anna?'

She nodded. The hairs on her legs stood on end. She did not know what to do with her body. She watched him drink her tea but now she wanted it. She didn't know how to ask. His rough cheeks sprouted grey stubble where he hadn't shaved himself and scabbed cuts where he had. Hairs poked through moles on his neck. His hands were tanned dark brown and covered in blotches. His skin sat wrinkled over raised veins.

'Can I have my ice?'

He reached into his pocket and counted out four pennies. 'Will you get a cone?' he asked.

'If they have it.'

He stayed standing by the railings, his hair blowing about his forehead, a splash of tea wetting the shirt he'd pulled on. Anna ran across the road.

The name on the sign was Italian. Extravagantly, unapologetically Italian. She had not known there were Italians in Wales, who owned shops and thought to paint their names on the main drag. She read the board of ices. All but two were crossed out. She buttoned her cardigan over her chest and hips. Pulled strands of hair off her face.

She could not remember the English for cone. Only the words for ice cream. There had been no ice cream in the countryside. Only apple cake, bad scones and bara brith they made at home. She thought she knew the Welsh. Something to do with chickens. Iar? Ia? Ya? She stared at the slim, brown-haired man serving. Did he speak Welsh?

When she came to the front of the queue she placed four pennies on the top of the counter and pointed to the painting on the left of the board above their heads. The slim man, all acute angles and white cotton, pointed to the picture as well.

'You want a cone?' he asked her. His accent was neither English nor Welsh.

She nodded. He slipped the little block out of its wrapper and pressed it into the wafer. She attempted a smile. 'Thank you,' she told him, in a careful accent.

Through the front window she could see her father waiting for her. Watching the queue outside the shop. No joy in his expression.

She walked out into the sunshine and ran across the road again. Lifted the cone like a torch to make him smile.

He opened his mouth to speak and the words that flowed out of him were warm and welcoming. Liebe – schönes Monster – schlau und unheimlich. Love – beautiful monster – clever and secretive. He made her laugh with his funny insults, with his familiarity. As if he weren't afraid of her at all. She let the ice cream melt on her lips, run down her throat. She let his words wash over her.

He spoke. She swam.

Children, half-dressed, faces pink from running, clattered past their backs. 'Dewch a nofio!' Come on and swim!

The sweetness of the ice cream had reached all the way to her fingers and her toes. She thought she might float like a balloon.

'You're not listening,' he said to her, smiling.

'Keep talking,' she told him.

'Happy monster.'

She bit into the last of the ice cream, pushed her tongue into the cone. She saw him summon a story, she watched him bring it forth. She tuned the meaning out. She floated on her back.

'Die Welt ist…' he was saying when he stopped. The world is…

'The world is out of sorts,' she told him.

'Out of sorts?' He didn't know the phrase.

'Isn't it?' she asked. 'The wrong way up. We're standing the way we're meant to but somebody has turned the world upon its head.'

He stopped and looked at her; a severe, searching gaze. She thought she had offended him. He looked out towards the sea. Down there, on the stones, her mother smoothed the blanket out and waited for them both.

Her father pointed towards the sky. 'The world is up there. But. You know… in pieces.'

Anna turned her back on the sea and stared at the row of shops, houses, hotels. The flags which rattled on their poles. The tea shop and the ice cream shop. The white paint that flaked on the façade of buildings whipped by a salty wind.

'There is something kindling in the window of the ice cream shop,' she said. Her father looked round to where she pointed, up there above the painted sign. 'At first, we can hardly see the smoke and it smells a little like cigarettes. The rooms get foggy. The edges of the windows blacken. The people start to run outside.

'You can see the curtains burning. The smell is stronger now. Like a bonfire. The window frames are burning, paint peeling and going black. Glass shatters and falls down. More people run, people disappearing in the distance, bodies getting smaller now. We can hear sirens. The flames are on the outside. Not just this shop. This one and the ones on either side, and the shop next to that one, on and on. The blackness spreading and sliding, creeping over every surface.'

Her father looked at her. 'You saw this?'

'They bombed the air base.' She waved a hand towards imaginary flames. 'Which I suppose means that we bombed the air base. But I don't remember having much to do with it.'

'Well, no,' her father said.

'Do you ever get scared,' Anna asked him, 'that people will hate you?'

He smiled awkwardly. 'All the time. But then it gets tiring. And what is one to do? I pull the blind down.'

'Like shutting your eyes?'

'I choose what I see. One day, Anna, you will find the world exhausting. But you will also find that you still have to live in it.'

'Was the ice cream instead of chips?' she asked him.

'I think it probably was,' he told her. 'Can we go and buy me some Capstans? The cold is getting into my bones.'

She nodded. Though she wasn't sure she wanted him inside a shop. They walked to a newsagent, on the corner of a little street which ran between two imposing boarding houses. Anna's eyes ran over her father's uncombed hair. His still damp shirt. His badly shaved complexion. In a shop, they would hear him speak. Still, though, there was an Italian name over the ice cream place and a queue which stretched out of the door.

The bell rang as they entered. An old man, with white strands falling from his bald head sat behind the counter reading the *Daily Herald*. He glanced up as they entered, then went back to his paper without saying hello.

On the wall behind him were shelves piled neatly with cigarette packets, books of matches, pouches of tobacco, and boxes of Frog model planes, all different kinds.

Her father pointed to the planes. 'Very nice,' he told her, in English.

She smiled and put her hand in his. The man looked up from his paper and held her father in a steady, wary gaze.

'A packet of Capstan, please, and how much for the planes?' her father asked.

The man behind the counter kept staring, then with one hand he reached behind him and found a packet of Capstan without looking. He put them on the counter and took up the dropped half of his newspaper.

'One shilling and six,' he said, glancing quickly down.

Anna felt her father hesitate. She looked at him and then at the packet and the man. She had been to the shop to buy him cigarettes more than once since he came home. She had never spent more than a shilling.

'Is that for the plane as well?' she asked.

'For the cigarettes,' the man said tightly, before her father could answer. 'That's how much they cost.'

Her father put his hand in his pocket and counted out the money. He placed the coins quietly on the counter and took up the packet where it lay. He touched a hand to her arm and they left the shop in silence. They crossed back to the beach side of the promenade and her father stopped to light his cigarette. Anna stood rigid and wondered if she had made it happen. Had wanted for the world to prove her right.

'I'm sorry about your plane,' her father said.

She shook her head. 'That's okay. I'm tired. We could just sit on the beach.'

There were more people in the sea now. The afternoon had grown brighter. The sun basked in a large patch of blue. The white stones on the beach shimmered, glinted and seemed to reflect the light. Anna unbuttoned her cardigan. She watched her father smoke. She wondered if the Italian man had taken his name down during the war. And, if he had, when he had put it back up. She patted her father lightly where his hand held the top bar of the railing.

'I like it when you speak,' she said.

Her father drew on his cigarette. His stubbled cheeks wrinkled and sprang back. Her mother waved to them. They both waved back. The wind put billow in the flags.

At Friday Club

Ralph Bolland

'Shit the bed!' muttered Eirwyn: head down, wiry old calves pumping uphill through frost-tipped bracken. The birds hadn't yet cleared their throats. A *wolf*? *Christ!* But still, with nostrils prickling in the sharp air, it was all he could think of. Hadn't dared say a word to Mair before leaving – she'd know by now he was gone. *By damn.* And the woman only just back on her feet.

When he stumbled back down from the field the night before, she had checked his temperature and set him on the sofa with a hot whisky.

'I said I'd call the Girl about now,' Mair told him. 'Don't want to miss her. It's a day in bed tomorrow or you'll be out for a while like I was.'

'Ahy,' mumbled Eirwyn.

What then could he have told her this morning? That he felt *better*? That he had to check if the brute was still there? Eirwyn groped for the baler knife in his old coat pocket. *As if. Planning to gut the thing?* But he had to check; had to know.

Tomorrow was Friday Club and the matter needed raising then. No fooling the boys.

He'd lain on the sofa, drifting and clammy, while Mair chatted to the Girl on the phone in the hallway. The *Girl*. Eirwyn had always envisaged her coming straight home on giving up her student flat: she was young enough still to take on the farm.

When he next woke, fevered and dull, his tiny wife towered above him holding a bowl of stew.

'She's moving in with her lad next month. Northampton.'

'Ahy,' said Eirwyn, momentarily unsure of his whereabouts; struggling to place Northampton, and with news of his own.

'I saw a wolf tonight, girl.'

Mair lifted her chin. 'A *wolf*?'

'Ahy. Up near the Common.'

Eirwyn was still wondering *what lad?* as Mair went to call the doctor.

And yet as he lay there, the exact order of things in recall – the *now* and the *then* – bamboozled him. He remembered lying on that same sofa, the Girl – just a toddler – cwtched in beside him; both with the winter vomits; set up in front of the telly with a bucket, a blanket and a favourite video – *Looney Tunes*. The antics of the hapless wolf (*was it a wolf?*) would have the Girl throw back her head, convulsing with laughter. Eirwyn had work to do, sure, but could have lain there till all the world fell in on itself; him laughing at the Girl as the Girl laughed at the wolf. *Not a care in the world. Was that ever me?* he'd thought.

*

The steep hill – more craggy wood than field – led up to Fron Common at the top. Eirwyn rarely had sheep up there these days – too much work on foot – and if he dared jump onto the quad, he'd surely bring on that nagging in the bollocks he'd been trying to ignore.

Still, that's where the beast had been last night. Through falling dusk, Eirwyn had spied something in the corner of his eye, but as he turned it was gone. (Mair would lament his

97

mucky specs.) *There!* Not there. Uneasy now, the light more like smoke, Eirwyn began breathing harder; a blue-grey shadow teasing him through the tree line. He held his nerve against the vague impression of something on hind legs twenty yards off. *A browser?* No deer round here. Someone's goat loose? The buggers were resourceful, he knew. *There again!* And Eirwyn looked directly into a pair of glinting, orange eyes; his own heartbeat acutely felt in his ears. The creature turned out from the lee of a pine and faced him brazenly, opening its body to present a fine white ruff, a smile blazing with mischief and pendulous manhood. Eirwyn gasped, then startled and stumbled briefly backwards, quickly gauging the direction of scarper. He scowled to himself and turned on down the track; a creeping, weary flush shrouding him as he hurried on home.

Had that been only yesterday? *Jesus.* Eirwyn struggled on up the rise. *A little out of puff, is all.* Fair play. Pushing seventy and had a bit of a scare. But *wolves*?

And it's not just the boys, is it? There's Helen too. Helen the Fron was making a decent fist of her dad's place. Old Philip had put a shell through the back of his own head two years before and everyone admired how Helen had managed the Fron since then. Not that anyone missed Old Philip. 'Carnaptious', is how Michael described him – and Friday Club would nod as one. But such talk stopped the first time Helen joined them for breakfast at Mick's Grill.

'You don't mind, boys?' she'd asked, drawing a chair from under the table. 'Always a shame Dad never went for Friday Club, I felt. He liked a breakfast. Why not? Once a week, talking shite with friends? Or even you lads. Hah! No – it would've done him good. Anyway, I'll be taking a different way at the Fron from now. My solemn word. Happy to be one of the boys. Full Welsh for me and a large cappuccino.'

What would Helen make of his wolf-talk? There was a simple question of decorum in one regard. And the other thing about Friday Club was Michael, and that forensic eye.

'You look pale,' Michael might say. 'Buggered up the VAT again, is it?'

There would be sniggers over sunny-side eggs and locally slaughtered sausage.

'Come on, Eirwyn, boy: something on your mind, as I see it.'

Nothing got past Friday Club. Like bloody fly-paper it was. Not that it wasn't the highlight of the week. It *was*.

Closer to the top Eirwyn was panting, a pool of sweat settling in the hollow of his neck. He had the sudden thought: *why didn't I get them over and show them the damn thing?* Friday Club would have had something to chew on. *Why not?* Well, in truth, others had tried to reschedule before. It had never gone well. Enmities lingered. *Don't fuck with Friday Club,* was the loose consensus. And what if the bastard thing didn't show? It's not like he had an appointment. Thirdly, he'd have had to tell Mair *why* the boys were coming over. And she would surely lift her chin.

No. As Eirwyn strode into the clearing his long legs surrendered power, swiftly and unexpectedly, and he knelt on the soft grass as if hamstrung; his glasses misted from his own breath. *They asked her to check for sepsis, by Christ!* And Mair so poorly this last while. *Get a grip! Wolves?* Friday Club would laugh.

And yet there it stood. Bold as gleaming brass. *Shit the bed*, thought Eirwyn. *I should have brought Friday Club.*

The creature was huge: stood on sinewy hind legs; shoulder leant casually against the giant stump of an old oak; arms folded across a barrel chest; one long foot draped *languorous* over the other. He wore a broad smile; those keen eyes fixed on Eirwyn, daring him to look elsewhere. Eirwyn dared not. He *had* yesterday when caught off-guard – the Wolf was unmistakably male. And *how!* Jesus. He would have to raise it at Friday Club.

'Eirwyn Wolf-slayer: as I live and breathe. You came for another look?' The Wolf chuckled in a louche baritone.

'Good morning,' said Eirwyn. 'I wanted to be sure… of what I'd seen.'

'And you brought a weapon?'

How did he know? Eirwyn, still light-headed, toying the weight of the baler knife in his pocket, quickly realised he wasn't scared.

'I'm a farmer. I mean no harm.'

The Wolf laughed again, not unkindly.

'Is it sheep you're after?' Eirwyn asked, at which the beast sighed then gently resumed his chuckling.

*

Come Friday morning, Eirwyn rebuffed Mair's protestations and had her drop him off in town. Fair play, Friday Club gave him complete attention. Eirwyn had a love for these men. (He'd said as much to Mair one evening, two glasses into Billy Bowen's cider. She reminded him the morning after and though Eirwyn did not recall saying it, he was both pleased he had, and pleased he'd forgotten.) Eirwyn relayed his wolf-encounters to the stunned assembly. A rare Friday Club silence held for a minute or more. Then followed an unseemly barrage:

'Describe it for us, Ery boy?'

'It's hard, lads. Not sure where to begin.'

'Try!'

'A big fellow?'

'Huge, Michael. Bloody ginormous.'

'How long would you say?'

'You mean, how high, Billy?'

'How HIGH? He was stood up?'

'He was bloody stood up, boys.'

'I'll be damned.'

'Bold as you like, this one, fellas!'

There was a chorus of *yea's* and *ahy's* until Michael drew the focus again.

'Have you lost any ewes?'

'Not a one. He's not after ewes.'

'Listen to yourself. He's a bloody wolf.'

'Danny's right. You have four-hundred head out there and a wolf the size of a fucking Christmas tree. What else is he after?'

'You have him wrong, lads. I asked that question.'

There were fast glances round the table.

'You *spoke* to the beast?'

'Ahy.' Eirwyn took a glug of coffee. Helen hadn't said a word. 'For about ten minutes. It was strange, boys, because... he knew things, see?'

'What things?'

'That I had a knife in my pocket, for one.'

'Might have been a guess. What else?'

'Which pocket; what kind of knife; was it for Xmas; other stuff.'

'Wolves are clever. Always have been.'

'Ahy. Could be guesswork.'

'Boys!' said Michael. 'What else did he know, Eirwyn lad?'

'Mair's name; both our ages, size of the farm, the Girl up at University; stock numbers, layout of the town, you boys too – and your business!'

Friday Club was cooking. Eirwyn lowered his voice.

'He asked about Friday Club; mentioned Old Philip too – knew all the details. No offence, Helen.'

'None taken,' said Helen. 'He sounds quite a beast.'

'You should have seen him, girl! No, perhaps not.'

Helen was quick to meet Eirwyn's eye. 'Why not, lad?'

'I mean… in some respects… it might not be for the ladies.'

Danny Griffiths toyed with his cutlery. Seeming to share Eirwyn's discomfort. But he couldn't know why.

'Eirwyn,' said Helen. 'I have four children.'

'You're among friends, Eirwyn,' said Michael.

Eirwyn closed his eyes and absently began to massage his temples.

'It's… what he was wearing, see?'

'Wearing!' said Friday Club in unison.

'What was he wearing?'

'Nothing but a smile, boys. He was in the buffo. BIG lad too. Not wanting in the old bedroom department.' Through a longer silence, Eirwyn found himself on the verge of tears.

'What does he want, I wonder?' Michael might have been puzzling his crossword, but Eirwyn felt a sudden unease: was Friday Club humouring him?

'I've no idea,' said Eirwyn. 'Helen. I'm sorry.'

'You've had a shock, boy,' said Helen. 'No apology necessary,' and she nodded briefly to Eirwyn. 'But I'd say the first thing this fellow wants is a decent pair of pants.'

Danny clanked his cutlery on to the plate and looked at Helen aghast. As Helen began to laugh Eirwyn thought she sounded just like the Wolf.

*

Helen's seamless slotting into Friday Club should have surprised no one. They were a motley bunch, led by Michael – the widower-intellectual and assiduous reader of the big papers – whose foresight and easy charm had brought them together. Billy Bowen could be an arse. He talked too much, too often and for too long about very little, but worked hard and honest for whoever asked. He'd lost half an ear in a rugby maul years before though liked to insist it was a chainsaw mishap. Once drunk Billy would confuse himself in the telling, but with such conviction that no one now was certain of the truth. Danny Griffiths was 'the boy' at 62. He had three strapping sons; the two eldest as ready to take on running their dad's farm as they were to paint their 18-stone frames pink and run down the High Street wearing only beer hats and mankinis to win a one-pint bet. When Danny's youngest lad emerged as the driving force behind the town's inaugural Gay Pride event, it had stoked feisty local debate. But Danny won much respect – and perhaps surprised himself – when he assured Friday Club that he would stand and cheer his estranged son all the way along the route.

'What would Jesus do?' Danny had asked. No one had ever seen Danny as a Jesus sort-of-bloke, but Friday Club thought it a good point, nonetheless.

*

The beast glanced over Eirwyn's shoulder, down towards the farmhouse. If someone was coming up the lane, Eirwyn prayed it wasn't one of the boys. They would surely talk to Mair and then the game would be up, but he saw no one approaching. When he turned back the Wolf was coolly perched atop the oak stump – it had to be twelve-foot high. How did he *do* that? The old farmer strained to avert his eyes.

'How's the Girl?' asked the Wolf, throwing Eirwyn completely.

The Girl, set to graduate, had decided Anthropology would *not* be her chosen career. Eirwyn was as baffled by this as he was soft putty in Mair's hands.

'Work has changed,' his wife had said. 'Look how she's blossomed at Uni. I wish I'd had that opportunity.' Eirwyn eyed his wife gormlessly and Mair waited a moment before adding, 'You're meant to say: "Oh, you were clever enough, girl."'

But right here and now, their Girl was none of this creature's business.

'She'll be home soon enough.'

'That's nice,' said the Wolf. 'From Northampton?'

'What's that to do with you?' Eirwyn snapped, but instantly regretted it. The Wolf had spoken pleasantly. Good manners were cheap.

'They won't believe you, Eirwyn.' His voice had a soothing music to it. Eirwyn wondered if Danny might use him in the Choir.

'Friday Club, I mean,' prompted the Wolf. 'They won't believe you about me.'

'Who said I'd tell them?' Eirwyn bridled. 'Who's talking about you?'

'Eirwyn,' said the Wolf affably, casually folding one long leg over the other which served to dim the priapic glare. Eirwyn had to stop himself saying 'thank you'.

'Then let's talk about you,' said the Wolf.

Eirwyn felt no threat at all and even pondered fleetingly whether the beast was *protecting* him. He slipped carelessly from his knees until he was sitting slightly askew on the grass like some tipsy picnicker.

'Eirwyn, Eirwyn,' said the Wolf. 'Talk to me, lad.'

Eirwyn raised his gaze to meet the Wolf's, exhaled a weary breath and closed his eyes. He wondered if the Wolf might offer him a cuddle, then to his own surprise, he opened up like a silage bag to the knife.

'It's Mair, see? If she goes before me...' Eirwyn paused, but the Wolf *was* listening. He explained just how ill Mair had been.

'Pneumonia. But you probably knew that, hm?'

Wolfy said nothing. Eirwyn considered this the mark of a good listener. He insisted that selling the farm hadn't even occurred to him until Mair fell ill. Now there was little room in his head for anything else.

'If I'm due an aneurysm, Wolf-lad, it'll start on that thought.'

And *if* they were to sell the farm: who would buy it? What kind of people? For what purpose? 'Rewilding' was a matter that had exercised Friday Club considerably: the bringing back of beaver and lynx; bears, wolves...

'No offence, lad!' Eirwyn opened his eyes, momentarily alarmed, but Wolfy sat rapt and unfazed. *He could be doing Yoga. A specimen of nature, he surely is. If only Michael was here.* Eirwyn's thoughts flitted on, bird-like.

'These humongous windfarms peppering the hills – pissing out sad trickles of electricity.' Hitting his stride, he asked Wolfy who did vegans think grew all the carrots? He rolled his palm in the damp clay at his side. 'This hill soil's no good for crops. Grazing is best. Better a nice bit of real lamb reared nearby than a chunk of soya flown in from where the Amazon forest used to be. No?'

Eirwyn spoke about bovine TB and badgers: 'People hate us for that.' And he spoke about hunting: 'I never rode horses, boy, but if a predator is taking your lambs?' He spoke about tuition fees: 'Why spend four YEARS studying something you'll never *do*?' He spoke of long hours, happy toil in the fields, and the acres of time he had to ponder things. He spoke as he never had. And Wolfy listened.

'Helen the Fron told me she wished she'd confiscated her dad's shotgun. Ahy! Like a little kid, not to be trusted with it. And there's one "Old Philip" happening every bloody week now. Is that in the news? If that was a policeman or a teacher? Imagine one politician killed themself every week.'

Eirwyn's eyes opened slowly, red-rimmed now, imploring his listener to make sense of the senseless. Noble Wolf gazed back: ears keen; majestic, bushed tail fitfully swishing the air around the oak stump. Eirwyn felt *worthy* of this creature's attention. (He would never dream of burdening Mair or Michael with this stuff.) Wolfy put Eirwyn in mind of the photographs of religious imagery the Girl used to send back from her travels: a peasant's roadside shrine; a series of exquisite icons adorning the walls of some vast Orthodox cathedral. *What a magnificent creature*. A few quick beads of sweat rolled off his brow and on to his lap. His teeth chattering, he had one last thing to say.

'Where's the bloody sense, Wolf, in a woman spending fifty years of cooking, raising kids and the rest when – *just* when she should be pottering with grandkids – she finds the man she's kept all this time is a burden only, bent over or lame, the best of him cut off, and good for nothing? What return is that for an old girl?'

Abruptly, Eirwyn ran out of steam. A breeze picked its way through the clearing. A sharp chill pierced his ribs. Wolf leant forward, an elbow on his lap, his chin on a fist.

'You've said this to Friday Club?'

'Ahy.'

Wolfy raised an eyebrow.

'Not in those words. I mean... they talk about it, but...'

'*You* don't say much?'

'Ahy. That's it.'

'Isn't that the point of Friday Club?'

'Ahy. That's it.'

'Tomorrow then?'

'Ahy.'

'Ahy,' said Wolf, mimicking Eirwyn, holding his gaze until the farmer looked away.

*

But the following morning at Mick's Grill, this promised unburdening of the soul didn't happen. Eirwyn knew it would come at a cost. He was foggy-headed and flagging under scrutiny. *Should have skipped the coffee. Now I've let Wolf down too.* And Billy was asking a question.

'But who would let a wolf loose up on the Fron?'

It wasn't a serious question. Billy tended to be less curious for answers than he was keen to sound considered and wise.

'Wasn't a dog, Ery? A big one: wolfhound or something?'

But Michael, who *was* considered and wise, had Billy Bowen's measure.

'Well,' he said. 'It doesn't matter, Billy, whether it was a dog, a wolf or a bloody Bengal tiger, does it? The bastard thing was talking to him!'

Billy's pissing-off of friends was a Friday Club staple. Eirwyn liked Billy most days, but here and now, under Friday Club's gaze, he liked Billy less. Eirwyn allowed his mind to wander, hoping to block out Billy's ratty quizzing. As Helen stood to go to the loo, he considered the pattern on her skirt. He had noticed it when she came in. *Paisley.* But it was not so much the design as the fact of there being a skirt at Friday Club at all. Eirwyn had missed two Fridays for Mair's illness, so maybe Helen wore the skirt then and the boys were used to it? He had hated missing those weeks and briefly caught himself resenting Mair for it. *By damn, boy. You're ruining everything.*

Then from nothing he had in his head an image of Helen wrestling a sheep. It was the nature of their work: sorting, marking, dipping, shearing. You spent time hauling stock: it was messy and heavy, could not be done in a skirt. Helen never had – nor would – but still it popped into his head: Helen the Fron in a mucky pen packed with flighty ewes and clad in that pretty skirt. Eirwyn worried the item might be ruined for a start. *We're not spoilt for clothes shops round here.* And perhaps it had been a gift? A token of affection? *Who from?* Worse yet: what if the skirt rode up? It would likely happen given the nature of the work. *What then, boy?* Oh. *Oh, indeed!* That posed questions of what might get to be seen and how Helen was set up downstairs.

Then, just as horribly, it wasn't Helen, but himself in the pen. Wearing Helen's pretty skirt, his arse covered in mud and shit, facing down a lusty tup. And what were *his* old pants like? The ram was bearing down on him, set to take care of business.

NO! *By damn!* No one would work sheep in a skirt, not him and not Helen the Fron. He had seen Helen wrestle sheep, and well enough she handled it. Eirwyn's chest was hammering. He'd never had such thoughts.

'Eirwyn?' said Michael.

Only now he *had*, see. And at Friday Club. With Helen herself walking back from the Ladies. Michael had spoken softly, but all eyes were on Eirwyn.

'You should get up the road? Back to bed, eh?'

Billy looked sheepish. Helen wore a benevolent smile. *Can she tell?*

'Ahy. Mair dropped me off. I wasn't up to driving.'

'No, I'd say. I'll get you back,' said Michael. 'All done here.'

Where was Danny Griffiths? Eirwyn couldn't recall him leaving. How long had he been dreaming? It was a nightmare. Eirwyn nodded, glad of the offer.

'But next week,' he said anxiously, 'you'll all come over. Up to the Common?'

There was a ready round of assents. Perhaps too ready.

*

The tripmeter on Michael's Nissan pick-up read 117, 501. The wide assumption was that, had the gauge run to seven figures, there would be another '1' at the beginning. Its resilience was legendary, and Michael tended it like a racehorse. As they traversed the back roads up above and behind the town, the two friends hardly spoke. Neither wore a seat belt; both casually ensconced on old, hard seats that knew their forms. The engine led a gruff chatter that stood in for small talk, climbing the lane past fields of sheep marked with a green 'EW' for 'Eirwyn Williams'. The joke was that each time Eirwyn took to spraying the word 'EWE' on a sheep (for the benefit of English tourists) he would always forget the spelling and give up.

Eirwyn's flock perked their heads up in woolly ensemble at the thrum of the engine. Michael pulled in by the lower shed, some way short of the farmhouse, and set his handbrake, the engine idling. They could have been sat in a parlour, whisky in hand, after a day's gathering.

'Wolves?' Michael asked, without judgement.

'Ahy,' said Eirwyn. 'Just the one.'

'You'd know him if you saw him again?'

'Ahy.'

'By damn.' Michael smiled. Both men looking out front. 'What's Mair saying?'

'She's absolutely delighted,' grunted Eirwyn and Michael chuckled as his old friend cranked open the truck door.

'Appreciate the lift, Mikey.' Michael nodded. Eirwyn looked towards him quickly: 'The boys will come over Friday, though?'

Michael inhaled deeply, having expected the question.

'Now well... there's a bloody thing, see, Ery. I thought they behaved well this morning. In the circumstances...'

'Circumstances?'

'Ahy. Those being, that either one of the lads is very poorly...' Michael hesitated. Michael – who was never lost for the right word. He found himself nodding gently to the purr of the engine.

'Or?' asked Eirwyn.

'Or,' Michael sighed. 'Or we have a bloody great cartoon wolf roaming free up the Fron Common.' He rubbed his eyes, rolled down the window. 'Seems a strange set of circumstances, does it not?'

'Ahy,' said Eirwyn. 'It does.'

'I think you should get some rest, boy, is what I think.'

Up ahead Mair was stood out from the house on the lane, looking down towards them. Michael popped his hand out the window and waved. Mair nodded back. Eirwyn was half-stuck in the doorway of the Nissan.

'Thank you, Michael,' she called. Michael lifted his hand again and Eirwyn knew at once that the two had spoken.

'Same fellow both times?' enquired Michael.

'Ahy.'

'Least we know it's not a pack, eh?'

Michael looked quickly to the dashboard: a sudden, uneasy spluttering from his beloved truck. *No.* He turned to see

110

Eirwyn neither in the vehicle, nor out; chin on his chest and one leg tottering on the path; the rest of his frame heaving and buckling against the side of the 4x4, snot trailing from his face. Through the windscreen Michael saw Mair's anxious stumble towards her husband and, as he got himself quickly out the truck, his own thoughts turned at once, and again, to Old Philip, who had not had someone like Mair around.

Fat Slug Lady

Sian Hughes

He is nowhere to be seen when she wakes. It takes her a minute to process his absence, and even then, whilst on a cognitive level she understands he's no longer there, her emotions are slower to surface, as if she were trying to summon an emotional reaction to a distant disaster. She takes an inventory of objects inside the tank: the cuttlefish bone glowing like a sliver of fallen moon, the plant pot that serves as a sanctuary, the rock, the fern, the dish, as if she could count him back into existence. When that fails, she turns to the area outside the tank, taking in the spray bottle used to keep the tank moist, the jar of beetroot and mealworm blend on the drawers, the lid. She stops to stare again at the lid, propped against the wall. Earlier, after feeding him wilted dandelion leaves from the windowsill, she must have forgotten to place the lid back on the tank. Forgetfulness was a symptom of her condition, a fog that sat on her brainstem like a toad; so whilst it wasn't the first time she'd neglected to replace the lid, it was the first time she'd woken to find him missing.

'Wilbur, where have you gone?' she says.

Talking to him was of course idiotic, even when he was there. He was deaf and pretty much blind, existing in a world of touch and shifting shadows. Yet she talked to him as often as possible, hoping he might recognise, in the scent of her voice, the print of her breath, the chemical shape of certain words. Heaving herself into a sitting position, she dangles her legs over the waterbed, exhausted already by the effort.

Lowering her legs to the floor, the unexpected warmth of the bare floorboards catches her off guard, however. So much time has passed since anybody touched her, aside from Carla, the physiotherapist. The wood feels alive beneath her soles, pulsing in sync with her body. Drawing strength from this visceral exchange, she stands up more quickly than usual, her gaze fixed on something she hasn't noticed until now: a silver snail trail, leading directly towards the half-open bedroom door.

*

She'd bought Wilbur at CJ's reptile shop in the Hafod, a year earlier, not long after the onset of her condition. In the beginning, she'd wanted a fish, but the fish moved too fast around their tanks, overwrought and unsettled, like thoughts that you couldn't hold on to. As if reading her mind, a woman in her sixties nursing a bloated belly, pink elbows, had risen from the gloom behind the counter.

'There's more out back. Come.'

In a squalid back office, a row of tanks hosted a variety of exotic animals: bearded dragons, hissing cockroaches, spiderlings. In a see-through box, with its shell barely visible beneath the peat, was a snail: a giant African land snail.

'They're not easy,' said the woman, seeing Joy stare. 'You need a heat pad and light bulb for starters. And they're not friendly. Quite the opposite.'

Joy wasn't looking for friendliness. Joy was looking for company, compatibility, synchronicity. As the snail reached a tentacle through the peat, picking up on Joy's frequency, Joy remembered a project on the life cycle of snails she'd done in junior school, twenty years earlier: shaded anatomical drawings that detailed the multiple, flickering chambers of a snail's heart bag.

'No worries. I'll take him,' she'd said.

*

Joy grips the bedpost more tightly, disoriented by the sight of the slime trail. Leaving the house was unthinkable. Whilst she could just about haul herself from one room to another in the flat, walking outside would be like treading through swamp water. And yet Wilbur was more than a pet. He was her soulmate, her mentor, and then some. So profoundly did Joy identify with his need to process the world in tiny increments, to linger forgetfully in one place, she worried she would die of loneliness if he vanished.

Sweat beads up in the small of her back as she proceeds towards the bedroom door. If he could do it, then so could she. Besides, in the four hours she'd been asleep, from six until ten o' clock, he couldn't have roamed further than the courtyard garden at the back of their building.

As she steps into the landing however, a soupy yellow light washes over her, as if she were stepping into the atmosphere of an unbreathable, distant planet. Below her, at the bottom of the staircase, a man emerges from his ground floor flat into the lobby. Joy lifts her arm in a half wave; pictures fucking the man in the stairwell. Her nightdress clings like fly-paper to her body, marking out the shape of her. But when the man's mouth forms a hole to say hi, Joy's arm crashes limply to her side. Mouthing something inaudible back, she retreats to the bedroom. Talking was even more fatiguing than walking; she could never make words mean what she wanted them to mean. A low-frequency hum vibrates through the cavity walls, tunnelling into her eardrums, as she makes the long, dismal journey back to her waterbed.

*

Joy hadn't always been this tired of course. Only two years earlier, she'd been working as a phlebotomist in a teaching hospital, training for the 10K at weekends. The 10K was her ex-partner John's idea, an A-type thirty-three-year-old who traded in futures and mainlined on Modafinil to get through. But not long after a needle-stick injury at work, a virus found its way into her body, and boom, that was that. She couldn't stand for longer than a minute without a churning dizziness brewing behind her eyes. She had a constant sore throat, aching joints, and worst of all, a nagging feeling of having forgotten something – or someone. John, who considered himself a health guru despite his amphetamine habit was supportive in the beginning, ordering kefir milk to support her gut flora, and explaining, in detail, the health risks of an unbalanced vaginal microbiome. However, after an awkward attempt at sexual intercourse in which he'd ejaculated prematurely, he'd announced her malaise was psychological.

'It's an avoidance tactic, you need to sort it,' he'd said. And then, out of nowhere: 'I've signed myself up for Iron Man.'

His ribs had the stripped-back quality of sanded wood; a spreading gap between his ribcage made it appear as if something might lunge out. In the months after her illness had taken hold, his weekends had been dominated by night-time cycling expeditions to mysterious destinations: places Joy couldn't find on Google maps.

'You're a quitter, Joy,' he'd added. 'You don't push through.'

They'd split up a few short months later, after she was referred to the rheumatology ward at the hospital, having temporarily lost the ability to swallow food. John didn't visit her until the third day of her stay, arriving minutes before the end of visiting hours in fluorescent bib tights and cycling gloves.

'Leave if you want to,' she'd said, when she could see how much it repulsed him to watch her sip from a beaker of puréed fruit.

'It's frustrating, is all. You have the power to heal yourself, everyone does. You *choose* negativity instead.'

She'd guzzled more purée through the spout, making a dog-like grunting noise.

'They put something in the fruit mix, fucking delicious. Full fat cream. Straight from the tits of a cow. Want some?'

She had begun to enjoy being gross. Being gross felt like vengeance for something. Meanwhile, John looked as if he might be sick or else cry, as if she was drinking raw sewage, his penis an upside-down exclamation mark in his tights.

'This whole thing is getting boring, babes. No offence.'

'Guess it's over then,' she'd said.

*

Joy tapes her mouth shut with sleep strips, activating the white noise in her sleep mask. The best thing to do was take a nap, calmly await Wilbur's return. The exchange in the landing had undone her; she was terrified of risking a relapse. Besides, giant African land snails were territorial, returning to their resting sites at dawn.

But even as she tries to sleep, the tank grows larger at her side, leaking gallons of queasy, humid emptiness into the air.

Her mind travels back to the first few days of Wilbur's stay with her, when he'd glued himself like a chrysalis to the underside of the lid, fearful of being out in the open. On the third day, he'd made his way down, burrowing into the substrate, his tentacles trained on her face. It was a moment of visceral connection, silent acceptance, that prompted her to make him a promise – a promise she would always watch over him. Turning to the tank once again, she takes another inventory of the contents, this time looking for clues as to why he might have disappeared. Her eyes drift to the plant pot at the back, which usually rests on its side. The pot – designed to provide Wilbur with a hiding spot – is upright.

Driven by a fresh wave of guilt, Joy drags herself over towards the casement window overlooking the back lane. She'd cleaned out the pot a few days earlier. Had she forgotten to put it back the way it was? Leaning into the window, she zeroes in on the terrace of Victorian houses on the other side of the back lane, the drystone wall at the rear. What if, denied the sanctuary of the overturned pot, Wilbur had ventured into one of those other, unknown spaces? Joy studies the wall a second time, estimating it to be five foot in height. During her training for the 10K, her workouts entailed twelve reps of step-up box exercises designed to strengthen her core; climbing a wall would have been easy back then. So why not tonight? After reneging on her promise to Wilbur, it was the least she could do. But something cracks in Joy's mind as she ruminates: a circuit in her brain powers down. She imagines stepping over the wall into nothingness, her foot going down through the ground. Climbing a wall was out of the question. John was right. She was a quitter. A coward.

*

She'd first met John at a further ed college in her hometown, where she was studying Level 1 in Health and Social Care. She was twenty, still a virgin, preferring to fantasise about old-time movie stars rather than flirt with the real-life alpha boys who swaggered around chugging Monster cans. John hit on her immediately, leaving her a scrawled note in her pigeonhole inviting her for milkshake in Subway. He said he'd been drawn to her self-sufficiency; the way she was happy to eat alone in the cafeteria. Physically she was also his type. Blonde, skinny, with an interesting, androgynous look, and a dimple above her bum that blew his mind. His assessment of her was all wrong, of course. She was as needy as it was possible to be. As for the back dimple, it had a face of sorts, and collected moisture, and made her want to die. Even so, the fact that he saw her, or thought he saw her, mattered.

They'd had sex almost immediately after meeting, in a disabled toilet cubicle near the auditorium, whilst she held the greasy white grab rail. She enjoyed the attention, the soft-sharp feeling as he entered her, radiating outwards before dissipating; but it was nothing like she'd imagined. She'd imagined a precise 'before' and 'after' moment: the whole world flowing into her body in one go, fusing with her on a molecular level, leaving her feeling integrated, real, full of knowledge. Instead, she'd felt vaguely discombobulated, unable to work out what it meant.

*

Feeling her anxiety intensify, Joy slumps into an easy chair below the window and reaches for the weighted blanket draped over the armrest. The blanket was the only item of John's she still possessed: a sports compression blanket that flushed waste from his muscles. Typically, Joy relished the bone-crunching sound of the glass pellets inside the blanket as she worked them between her fingers to relieve stress: the numbing weight of fabric on her body. Now, the blanket serves only to remind her of her cowardice.

Outside the window, she hears men's voices – likely drug dealers. (After all, the back lane was a no-man's land that didn't appear on any of the deeds belonging to nearby houses.) She imagines a man's boot on Wilbur's shell, a tectonic, slow-motion cracking, yet something about the voices also stimulates her, and she recalls a summer when she and her younger brother created a 'Missing Cat' leaflet to distribute to folk in their cul-de-sac, after their kitten, Mr Goose, had gone awol. She wonders about creating a similar leaflet for Wilbur, enlisting the help of the community, an action that wouldn't entail leaving the flat.

Joy rifles through the bureau to find stationery, ignoring a new pain at the root of her hand. In the bottom drawer, she finds a pad of vintage graph paper like the paper she used for the snail project back in primary school; below it, an old orange pencil case. She would put the leaflet in the window overlooking the street. Taking the paper to the easy chair, she draws Wilbur's outline from memory, as fluently as if she were being guided by her unconscious. Beginning with an undulating line that sweeps up the paper to represent the edge of Wilbur's foot, she veers to the left to form a tail. Then, when the drawing is finished, she writes MISSING in Sharpie across the top.

*

She wakes at around six in the morning to flickers of laughter from the street, a single, flat bang on the front door that has the quality of a car backfiring. Going downstairs for the second time in one day, hoping that Wilbur has been found, that somebody has seen the leaflet in the window, a padded envelope awaits her on the doormat.

Joy brings the envelope to her nose. Since the diagnosis, she has taken to smelling things. A mineral smell hits her airways, making her organs curl in from the sides. Turning the envelope around to open the seal, a huddle of words grouped together on the flap comes in and out of focus as she climbs upstairs.

Fat Slug Lady.

Fat Slug Lady.

Fat Slug Lady.

Time slows – she forgets to breathe. At some point she opens the envelope, tipping the contents on the waterbed. Attached to the amber-white apex of what appears to be a shell remnant, a Post-it note reads:

'This Your Snail? Freak.'

Joy takes in the details of the smashed mantle, a substance like milk oozing out. The deceased snail is smaller than Wilbur, an ordinary garden snail, but with a glossy, lickable sheen. She expects to feel relief but doesn't. Turning to drink from the tumbler of stale water on her drawers, she recalls noticing something else among the debris. Pivoting slowly to face the bed again, her attention focuses on a cluster of small white spherical objects spilling from the snail's broken side, like snowberries. Joy teases out a sphere. The surface is semi-translucent, allowing her to see, as if through a fogged-up window, the dark, jellied embryo inside.

*

She'd gotten pregnant within a couple of months of meeting John, neither of them having bothered to take precautions.

Sharing the news with him in a noisy student pub, after college, he'd asked, casually, if it was 'his' or someone else's. Instead of being pissed off or hurt, she was flattered he thought her capable of seducing other men.

A fortnight later, he'd driven her to an abortion clinic, miles from the city.

'I think I want to keep it,' she'd said, suddenly, as they were stopped at a set of traffic lights before the turning. 'I'm not sure.'

She saw something half cross his face: the sort of expression a person makes when they pretend that they haven't seen you. A Toyota pick-up with a gleaming radiator grille beeped impatiently as they pulled away from the lights, and John, who had a black box fitted to his car to cut down on insurance, braked quickly to startle the driver.

'Stupid cunt,' he said, giving the driver – an older woman – the middle finger.

Joy hadn't raised the subject again. Besides, having a baby was a far-fetched, impossible thought, like deciding to free-climb El Capitan, or imagining oneself as a real, functioning adult. As they climbed the steps to the clinic's door, hand in hand, but with their palms barely touching, Joy was swamped by the strangest feeling ever, as if time was expanding and slowing down. She wondered who John was, who she was; her movements felt off and too slow.

'Let's get it over with,' said John.

*

Joy stows the dead snail in her pocket, swaddling it in tissues. She wonders about burying it by the beech tree, the only green part in the courtyard, where she once read a book in the sun.

But her core is weaker than ever, as though she swallowed a mouthful of space; as though the space has displaced all her innards. She hasn't thought about the termination in months, although perhaps the truth was that it was always coming back to her in other ways: as a taste in her mouth, a new symptom. At the time, she didn't regret her decision: reproducing was irresponsible and selfish given the environmental crisis, she'd have made a lousy, unmotivated mother. But then again, over time, perhaps her body had begun to feel otherwise. Perhaps her brain, in slowing everything down to the point where she could no longer function or metabolise energy, was trying to prevent bad things from ever happening again.

Tearing the MISSING leaflet from the window, she sits on the waterbed a while, more fearful for Wilbur's life than ever before. Over in the States, giant African land snails were considered pests. During rainy seasons, government officials were tasked with hunting them down one by one, throwing them whilst still alive in vast municipal fridges in the agricultural department. The barbarism of it shocked her, appalled her.

Something starts up in her foot, a constellation of pins and needles so uncomfortable she needs to press into the floor to make it stop. The pressure against her foot is a relief, anchoring her against the force of a new feeling that whips across the bottom of her lungs. A feeling close to anger.

*

Before she knows it, she is out in the back lane, with no memory of having descended the stairs or crossed the garden, fuelled by the same unfamiliar emotion. She remembers Carla, the physiotherapist, telling her how, a few years earlier, a neighbour tried in vain to transform the lane into a community area, hauling out a trestle table for a village 'Big Lunch', stringing battery fairy lights along the fuzzy damp capstones.

Increasing the brightness on her phone light, Joy searches along the verges inch by inch, as though she were a police investigator zoning out a crime scene. Afterwards, she scans the wall opposite in search of footholds; anything she might be able to use to lever herself over, into the terrace of gardens behind. Shining her light into the darkest sections, a tabby cat materialises from the undergrowth, like something from a picture book, or the past, shaking the night from his body.

Joy follows him through an arched doorway at the rear of the end house, where the door is very slightly ajar, into a creaturely, primeval-looking wilderness. Tall tree ferns, intersected by clumps of dark-stemmed bamboo canes populate one side of the garden, all of which run along the length of a boundary wall. Below them, plantain lilies and damply gleaming elephant ears spill onto a weed-sprung garden path. At the end of the path, illuminated by a glitching downlight is a garden pond, covered with a film of organic matter. Fearful of what might be underneath, Joy considers running back into the lane. But something stops her in her tracks.

The light, a lunar glimmer, is coming from an old brick wall on the other side of the garden; specifically, from a patchwork of crumbling lime render teeming with snails, their trails criss-crossing the surface like the lines in satellite images of earth from outer space. Joy's attention focusses on a pair of larger than average garden snails, wrapped around each other to mate, tasting each other's faces, each other's bodies. Even before her systemic collapse, John's A-type personality meant that a quickie was always his preferred route to orgasm, but perhaps the atrophying of their love life was as much to do with her as with him. Whilst John's way of avoiding bigger questions was to rush around on an accelerated schedule, with no time for connection nor remembering, Joy avoided issues by slowing down to the point where everything lost focus and meaning, like music played back at slower speeds.

Joy continues along the path towards a low wooden gate, drawn forwards as if by some weakly magnetic silver snail trail, oddly undeterred by the fact that Wilbur isn't on the wall with all the other snails. Beyond this gate, a second path runs the entire side of the house, illuminated by an LED sensor. Turning her phone light off, no need for extra light here, a sudden dread pools like groundwater in her stomach.

*

After the termination, Joy had just gotten on with life, retraining as a phlebotomist at community college. She liked practising late into the night on the dummy arms; the stink of ethyl alcohol got her high. One night, on her way home from work, she was swamped by the same feeling she'd experienced on her way to the abortion clinic a year earlier, dropping into slow motion mode without warning. John urged her to join his city gym, where a personal trainer recommended weighted plank exercises to jump start her metabolism. Six months later, when her metabolism had increased by less than five percent, she cancelled her gym membership.

A year or so later, by which time she had a job at the hospital, her finger grazed across the tip of a used sharp. Following protocol, she'd let it bleed freely, washing it with soap and water at the water station, organising for a tetanus booster at the surgery. The risks were minimal, she shouldn't have given the incident a second thought, but in the days that followed, it was as if a flock of birds were trapped inside her finger, flapping, slashing, growing; she sucked at the wound day and night. When her finger grew finally silent, the pain was replaced by generalised flu-like symptoms, exhaustion, so she took to her bed with all the medication she could lay her hands on, sleeping for hours at a time, dreaming of sleep while she slept. John said she needed protein: grass-fed hunks of flesh. But meat repulsed Joy to the core, not because of the taste, nor any environmental arguments, but because meat fed the shame that lived inside her.

*

Joy reaches the end of the path, where a six-foot-high timber gate opens onto a front garden so different from the back garden as to feel like a different world. A manicured lawn slopes gently towards a box hedge; there are borders full of late blooming flowers. Joy's first instinct is to keep to the wall, hide. But reminding herself that she is here to find and save Wilbur, she steps closer to the lawn. A three-tiered water feature, topped with a carving of a pergola, illuminates two minutely carved stone dancers. Beyond that, bent over in a pool of separate light, is a man. The dread in Joy's stomach quickly cools, like the materials of a star coalescing. The man is holding something in his hand, a canister of table salt, which he shakes up and down over the ground, scattering salt in huge arcing zigzags.

Joy knows what he's doing at once.

'Stop it!' she says. 'Just stop.'

The man becomes still for an instant, before spinning his head anticlockwise. He yells something back before standing, at which point Joy notices that he's also carrying a magnifying glass. At his feet, stranded on heaped mountains of white powder, are a pair of beautiful, picture book snails, bubbles of slime and air foaming around the frilled perimeter of their shells.

'Get off my property!'

The man marches across the garden towards her, the cylinder of table salt swinging from his hand like a police baton. In the time it takes him to cross the lawn, Joy takes in everything in the garden with microscopic clarity: the columns of white flowers bending in the breeze, the dancing couple on the water feature spinning in increments smaller than the individual degrees of a circle, the garden snails toppling, frame by frame. She should be scared but isn't. She has never felt this powerful, this alive.

The man reaches the edge of the lawn, where she's standing. Technically, Joy knows she's in the wrong, a deranged trespasser in a Disney nightdress, but she also knows that you could be wrong in a variety of ways. And suddenly, it's as if everything in Joy's life has been leading up to this point, the energy locked away in the mitochondria of her cells now available to her, redeemable. Grabbing the cylinder from the man's hand, she shakes salt into the soft blob of his face, over and over, as though she were spraying a magnum of champagne.

'How do you fucking like it?' she says.

The man leaps backwards, holding his face, giving Joy time to grab the snails.

*

It's light by the time she returns to the flat. Fuzzy green burs cling to her nightdress like confetti, her ankle throbs where she brushed against nettles, running down the path with the snails. In the bathroom, she picks off the seed burs one by one, before attending to the sludge under her fingernails: decomposing plant debris from the pond, where she'd tried – futilely – to rinse the salt from the snails' dying bodies. It had been impossible, of course. Impossible to reach beneath the shells; to halt the slow, lopsided horror of their melting. But at least she'd tried, at least she'd spoken up, so that even though she hadn't found Wilbur, she feels lighter, more whole than in a long time.

As she enters her bedroom a few minutes later, early morning sunshine filters through the front window blinds, and she remembers moving into this flat, this village, not long after her separation from John. It was the very last village in the county, with no connections to her previous life, no amenities apart from a spiritualist church housed in a shipping container on the green. Her plan had been simple: stay for six months, regain her strength, reapply for her job at the teaching hospital. Although she'd stayed longer than intended, she was perhaps closer to achieving that goal. Moving the weighted blanket from the floor, John's smell fills the air for a second, a smell with a vinegary bass note, like perfume exposed to sunlight. Tomorrow, she would take the blanket to the charity shop.

Finally, she glances over at the tank. Wilbur has still not returned, and Joy allows herself to consider the possibility that he may be dead – or gone. Even so, she moves closer to the glass, drawn to something. The substrate looks different from usual, the peat billowing up at the back of the tank like the windward side of a dune. Joy squats to sniff the glass, feeling the strain in her glutes. The tank has an earthier scent than usual, dustier, the humidity level on the hygrometer reading a low 55 percent. Leaving the lid off must have dried the peat.

Moving to the side of the terrarium, Joy uses her right hand to carefully sweep away layers from the built-up peat, compelled now to examine underneath. The peat vibrates to the rhythms of her touch, and whilst it takes her another few seconds to make visual contact, she can already sense the dreaming bulge of Wilbur's whorls, the brown bands that appear purple, or red, in a certain light.

'Wilbur,' she says. 'Why were you hiding?'

Joy lifts him gently from the tank, cupping her hands around his extravagant, unapologetic body. Unless the slime trail was older than she'd imagined, he must have left and come back. Inspecting his body for damage, she notices a new, silvery barrier across the opening of his shell, a sign of wintering. Maybe he'd been here all along? Aestivating. Waiting.

Transferring him temporarily to the shoebox that once contained her Nike air trainers, Joy lines it with layers of warm, damp tissue paper, before spraying the tank to correct the moisture levels. Finally, when the humidity value on the hygrometer reads a perfect 80 degrees, she deposits three chunks of cucumber on the peat, beside a shallow dish of cool, dechlorinated fresh water.

Fruits of Our Labour

Tess Powell

In June of this year a big California Bay Area Tech Company filed for bankruptcy. Its large headquarters in the downtown San Jose area wasted no time in sacking all its employees. They were sent out in a single file line with their belongings tied to a stick and slung over their shoulders. As soon as they were gone the hand of God came out of the sky to smash the structure to smithereens, and a large sign was placed out front that read 'Failure of Capitalism'.

Bonita, a thirty-year-old now former employee of this company, wasted no time wallowing. With no job there would be no rent. She lived in the downtown area and the only food stores nearby carried seven-dollar bananas and bespoke spinach sold by the leaf. She wouldn't kid herself that that lifestyle was one she could maintain. She broke her lease, left her downtown studio apartment and returned to her mother's house.

Her mother lived in an old two-bedroom bungalow in the Burbank neighbourhood that she bought fifty years ago for $20 and a blow job. It had useless dried-up front and back yards dotted with parched foliage.

Her mother opened the front door to see Bonita with her suitcase and didn't ask a single question. 'Well, come on in,' she said. She was 65 and still worked every day as a tax agent. 'It's shit,' she liked to say, 'but at least it's my shit.' Then she laughs and coughs and then sighs. Her retirement plans were,

'Don't have any,' and her aspirations were 'Who needs 'em.' Every day at 4 p.m. she smokes a cigarette in the backyard just in case she gets a little 'too lucky' with her health.

'Your old room's got some junk in it,' she said, pointing down the hallway past the kitchen. 'But don't move it because it's got nowhere else to go.'

Bonita went into her room with her bags then slumped down onto the floor.

'Me and the junk both,' she said to herself.

*

Job searching is a form of self-flagellation. Somehow, despite Bonita's experience, the bar to entry had moved further in only one month of being unemployed. She barely met the qualifications for tech jobs deemed entry level, and kept getting rejection emails suggesting she pad out her resumé.

At the three-month mark she got desperate and went to see a career counsellor to tell him what was missing.

'Elementary schoolers are doing a surprising amount of our web programming these days,' the counsellor said. 'They'll have ten years of experience by the time they finish high school.'

'Isn't that unethical? I mean, a violation of child labour laws?' Bonita asked.

He shook his head. 'It counts as after-school extra-curriculum these days.'

*

In spring, at the four-month mark, she looked outside her window to see wildflowers blooming and decided to take a walk. She realised she hadn't walked around her childhood neighbourhood in nearly ten years. A lot had changed. The older people who had lived there had either left or died, and younger couples that worked in high-paying jobs moved in. They painted their houses white, and repaved their driveways grey, and kept their grass a healthy bright green despite the drought. Most notably, every single one of them had a small lemon tree in their front gardens.

She didn't notice it at first. Citrus fruit trees were a common sight all over California, but there definitely weren't *this* many when she was growing up. Definitely not ones so uniform, so centrally placed and perfectly trimmed. She asked her mother about it at dinner.

'There's a neighbourhood association now. Uptight people. Candy cane lights at every house for Christmas, the same wreath at every door for Thanksgiving. They voted on every house having a lemon tree out front for aesthetics. Makes us more uniform, nicer, makes property values increase, I guess,' her mother said.

'But they can't just force people to do that stuff, right?' Bonita asked.

With her mouth full of food her mother replied, 'No, but they don't have to, everyone's pretty gung-ho for it.'

'Except you?'

She smiled. 'Except me.'

*

Bonita continued her routine of applying for jobs and taking walks. On one she slowed to watch a man prune his lemon tree. Its many fat lemons glistened perfect and yellow, threatening to fall off their stems. He gathered the ones that did and put them into his garden-waste bin along with the tree trimmings. His lawn was kept uniform and clear. She stood there and stared as he did this until he finally met her gaze and she hastily kept on walking.

It was Saturday. Other couples were out manicuring their shrubs and adjusting the sprinklers on their emerald lawns. They glanced at her as she walked by, for just a second too long. They must have known she wasn't like them, that she didn't belong. They had properties and careers and families. They had lemons, bobbing and shining like treasure; succulent and fat and rotting and dying and perfect.

At the end of her walk she came to a corner where one lemon tree hung over the edge of the sidewalk. Its fruit dangled within reach, so much of it, so ready to give, so many having fallen and scattered, rolled into the street. A sign had been nailed to its trunk that said, 'No picking'.

*

Under the dark cover of 3 a.m. she slinked out of the house dressed all in black. She felt ridiculous, she felt exuberant. She had pillowcases tied to her belt. One by one she approached the houses on her block and one by one picked all the lemons off their trees. They put up no fight as they slipped off their stems and into her bags. The plush grass of the lawns gave way under her feet and absorbed all sound. She smiled wildly, tying off one sack and starting on the other. With her side of the street entirely bare she felt satisfied and carted her lemon sacks back home where she stowed them in her mother's garage and hid them under a tarp.

Without even changing clothes she flopped down onto her bed, heart pounding, covering a laugh with her hands. She tossed in her bed thinking of every formative event in her life and every failure until she finally shut her eyes and fell asleep.

*

Bonita woke up several hours later with drool clinging to her lips and the sound of voices shouting. Then the memory of her early morning activities returned and she jolted upright. She blinked crust out of her eyes before stumbling up and over to the windows at the front of the house.

She peeked out the curtain to see several of her neighbours standing in a group and pointing back to their homes, their arms crossed, their expressions sour. Her heart beat faster. She nearly jumped out of her skin when her mother opened the door holding groceries.

'Damn weird thing happening out there,' her mother said, kicking off her shoes. 'Neighbours think we got some sort of lemon thief in our midst. Actin' like it's the end of the world as we know it.'

'Huh,' Bonita said then turned her attention back to the scene outside. The small group had finished working themselves up and were returning to their own houses, waving at each other, their eyes squinting. She thought she saw one of them look towards her and she jumped back from the window.

*

Later that afternoon while her mother was occupied playing online chess in her room, Bonita crept into the garage, climbed over the unused bicycles, lawn mower, boxes of old kitchenware, and peeled back the tarp to reveal the bulbous lumpy lemon sacks. She opened one.

The lemons glowed, impossibly golden. She picked one up and felt the textured surface of its skin, cool and firm. She laughed at the absurdity of what she had done. She had stolen all that fruit. She wasn't even sure what she was going to do with all of it. For now they would wait in her garage, and after a few days when the commotion had died down she promised herself she would haul them to a charity.

Bonita exhaled. 'Well, that's that,' she thought. Something weird to tell a stranger at a bar, something she could laugh about later with her future colleagues at her future job with future health insurance.

Then she heard dogs barking.

She stumbled a bit over the bags and went to the dirty garage window.

Outside, one of her neighbours was going down the street with two bloodhounds on a leash. They had their noses to the ground, sniffing fervently, their great big jowls slick with drool. The man who held them had a lemon in his other hand for them to sniff.

Bonita gripped the edge of the window and watched.

They came down the sidewalk, closer and closer then stopped briefly in front of her house.

Were they serious? Lemon-hunting dogs?

She thought maybe the jig was up but then the dogs changed direction and led the men to a house across the street and its lemon tree.

Of course they wouldn't be able to find the stolen lemons that way. There were lemons on every damn block.

She couldn't relax. She was boiling. It wasn't right. Why did it matter so much to them? They weren't even going to eat their own fruit! It was only the thought of their property in someone else's hands that made them so angry. That's why they couldn't let it slide.

Well, then, neither would she.

*

She went again. She waited several weeks until their guards had dropped, but she was sure someone would be watching this time: through video surveillance or paranoia-induced insomnia. She covered herself more, making sure you couldn't make out her face or build. She wore her mother's Neighbourhood Garden Association jacket, one that nearly everyone in the area had. They were given them as Christmas presents one year; meant to be worn while working in their yards during the colder months, in order to be more uniform and presentable of course. She hoped that even if she was seen, she would look just like any one of them.

She crept to the other nearby streets with her bags, and once again let all the ripe fruit fall effortlessly into them. Silently, so silently, on the soft grass with the dense cover of leaves. This time she filled up and deposited her lemons back home then went out again and again, until as many houses as she could reach were bare. At not quite sunrise she hurried back home, stripped off her clothes, got into bed, and slept until noon.

*

This time she woke to a harsh pounding at the door.

Her mother was away at her office so wasn't there to answer it. Bonita groggily sat up, but then, as the pounding continued, she shot out of bed. Out of the peephole she could see a man much older than her, crossing his arms and scowling.

Had she been found out?

No. If she had, these were the type of people who would assemble an angry mob to confront her. One man was nothing to fear. She hoped.

Bonita opened the door but the man was already walking away. On the doorstep she could see a note: 'Neighbourhood meeting tonight, 6 p.m. Corner Park'. Looking out she saw that others were knocking at doors on her street and leaving notes for those that didn't answer. One of them saw her and eyed her as she quickly slid back inside. The note held tight in her sweaty hand.

She asked her mother about it when she got home.

'I'm not going to that bullshit,' her mother said, and set her car keys on the kitchen table.

'But we might look guilty if we don't,' Bonita said. She really didn't want to go either, but she needed to. She had to see what it was they would talk about.

'Guilty of lemon thieving?' her mother said. 'Sure, why not.'

Bonita groaned, 'Mom, just – come on. I don't want to go alone.'

'No dice,' she said sipping cold left-over morning coffee and squinting at the daily crossword.

Bonita felt like whining then, like a kid, but she was 30.

*

Five minutes to six she walked to the corner park alone.

There was a large congregation already assembled of neatly dressed people with arms crossed and scowling faces, whose gazes darted around to everyone and anyone. At the head of the crowd, standing on top of a picnic bench, was who Bonita learned to be president of the Neighbourhood Association – Carl. He held a megaphone and had two women behind him standing with their arms crossed like bouncers.

Carl addressed the crowd with a sort of seriousness that

seemed commendable until you remembered what it was he was so serious about.

'Friends, neighbours, I'm sure you all know why we are gathered here today,' he said, sweeping an arm over the crowd. 'There is a glaring problem we must address, that is an insult to our community, a threat to our homes, and a devastation to our livelihoods. Most of you here have already been stolen from, and I feel your pain. By this morning mine and the property of twelve more houses had been usurped, and action must be taken.'

This is when the two women behind him pulled out large images that they each held up, turning slightly left and right to display them to the crowd. They were pictures of Bonita, blurry and low quality; you could not make out her face, but you could unmistakably see the Neighbourhood Association jacket that she had worn. She clenched her jaw and shoved her sweaty fists into her pockets.

The crowd let out a shocked gasp, some covering their mouths.

'Yes... I know it may come as a shock to you but unfortunately the culprit is one of our very own. It could very well be one of you here right now.'

Everyone threw glances this way and that, family groups huddling closer together as if exposure to such a deadly criminal would have some impact on their physical well-being.

Carl cleared his throat and then with a look of upmost sympathy he said, 'We have thought long and hard how to deal with this problem, and have concluded that a voluntary search of your homes may be necessary to unveil the criminal.'

At first the crowd seemed to agree. The suspicious neighbours should most definitely have their homes searched, for one of them was the culprit and they should be found and persecuted. But then it dawned on them that that meant their own homes would be searched as well.

'Well, is your home going to be searched?' one voice called out.

Carl seemed to be taken aback by this, 'Well... I don't see why that would have to be necessary. Everyone can see that I have been stolen from as well.'

'So have most of us!'

'You could have stolen from yourself as a cover-up!'

The crowd seemed to like this idea and Carl was left stuttering into the megaphone trying to defend himself. Bonita liked the implication that picking your own lemons was 'stealing' from yourself.

It became a free-for-all of accusations.

'I saw you out late last night in your jacket!'

'I've seen Pete pick his lemons before!'

'We should take alibis!'

'What about Annie Vertrees? She never even PUT a lemon tree in her yard!'

Bonita froze. That was her mother's name.

'She never does any of the neighbourhood association activities!'

'Yeah, and where is she now? She isn't here!'

There was some agreement in the crowd. They really liked that idea. Her mother was the odd one out, she was an easy target. Bonita wasn't sure if speaking up would make it better or worse. She wasn't even sure if anyone noticed her.

They didn't stick to the topic of her mother for long, as they continued with more in-fighting and accusations. Bonita used it as an opportunity to sneak away and make a beeline for home.

*

The following days were filled with chaos.

The neighbourhood had taken extreme measures to protect their lemon trees. Signs indicating alarms and cameras were set up at the front of lawns. Barbed wire was wrapped around the perimeter of lemon trees. Bear traps had been set up in the grass which were already resulting in many dead squirrels which some chose to string up and hang on their garden fences as a warning.

When Bonita had the chance and took a walk around the neighbourhood, she saw people eyeing her from windows, from folding chairs set out on front porches. This all culminated in her stopping to tie her shoe, standing back up, and seeing a man with a rifle slung over his shoulder standing in front of his house, looking so out of place with his polo shirt and thick glasses, but his finger rested on the trigger.

*

She felt hot. The muscles in her face ached from her scowl. She paced her kitchen over and over again, throwing her hands up, grumbling and cursing and wondering to herself how in the hell it could get so bad.

Would they kill her if they found the lemons stowed away in her garage?

How far were they willing to take this?

How much did it mean to them?

She clenched her hot hands open and closed and opened and closed them onto the cold tile of the kitchen counter. Then she grimaced, and that grimace became a smile.

She grabbed a bag of the stolen lemons and concealed them

in a box topped with some of the old junk in the garage, then hastily loaded the box into the back of her car. She drove to a post office a city over, in a poorer area where her neighbours wouldn't dare go. She crushed each lemon, spewing its seeds and innards into fresh-scented carnage, then stowed them in plastic shipping bags and addressed them to each one of her neighbours.

It took a day for the packages to arrive.

They were delivered one after the other, set onto front porches, and one by one they were brought inside.

Bonita had been watching all day from her window. She sat in the living room, unable to pull herself away. Her eyes just fixated on her neighbours' doors, her hands clammy, her eyes red.

Then they began to storm out of their homes and onto the street.

The first waved his box in the air with the lemon in his hand and was shouting obscenities until he was joined by another neighbour with his own lemon corpse. The ones who heard what was happening saw the packages and went to open their own, after which they immediately joined the chaos.

Bonita watched, her eyes unblinking.

What would they do now?

What would they do now?

They started fighting. Just shoving at first and then punching, pulling, slapping, kicking and then – BAM!

Bonita jumped. A gunshot was fired. For a moment her heart froze. Then she saw Carl, his gun pointed up to the sky. Everyone looked at him.

He said something that Bonita couldn't hear, but when he was done the crowd dispersed, going back into their own homes.

It couldn't be that easy, could it? What was it that he said to them?

She cursed under her breath and ran out the door to get a better look. Then from everywhere neighbours began emerging from their homes, going towards Carl's house carrying timber, old furniture, electric drills, nail guns, glue, rope. They moved through the back gate of his home and to his backyard. Their eyes were full of solemn focus. What in the world were they doing?

It wasn't until later that afternoon the gate to Carl's yard opened again, and from it a large structure was carried out.

A guillotine.

It was made of mismatched, different coloured parts all frankensteined together. Yet it looked sturdy. It looked effective. A large blade sat up top, sharp and glinting in the setting sun.

They brought it to the centre of the street, looking so out of place before the white painted houses with rose bushes and welcome mats.

They left it there like a beacon. Some came door to door, slipping notices into mail slots demanding that whoever was the culprit turn themselves over. That extreme measures might have to be taken for the betterment of the community otherwise.

Bonita crumpled the notice up in her hand.

Extreme measures were going to be taken.

But not just by them.

Bonita ran into the kitchen before she stopped dead in her tracks as her mother stood before her, the door to the garage open, a lemon in her hand.

'Bonita… what the hell is this?'

Bonita clenched and unclenched her fists.

'It's what it looks like, isn't it?' she answered, then shouldered past her mother, feeling undeterred. Getting caught didn't matter now.

'Bonita, stop it, what are you – what's going on with you?'

Bonita turned to face her mother, her eyes stinging.

'What's wrong with all of them? What's wrong with this neighbourhood? What's wrong with this – this world? I'm so tired, so tired of it. And you just – you do nothing! You never do anything!'

'Bonita—'

Bonita threw open the kitchen cabinets and began picking through them sloppily, letting things topple to the floor: Tupperware, decade-old candles, pasta boxes, forgotten bags of tea, until she reached the back. She pulled out a tattered old copy of *Joy of Cooking*.

'And you're going to die for it, Mom. You're going to suffer for it. Out there they'll mount your head on a pike. They'll parade it around the streets and no one will bat an eye.'

Her mother's face soured.

'If you want to go around being a lemon thief then fine, but what in the hell are you trying to accomplish?' She pounded the lemon down onto the table and then retreated down the hall to her room where she slammed the door.

Bonita didn't even look at her. She just threw the pages of the book around searching and searching – her mother's words were ringing in her ears. But then she found what she was looking for and yanked it out of the book. A recipe for devil's food cake. She began to bake.

Preheat the oven. Mix together the dry ingredients. Beat the butter with the sugar. Add eggs, add vanilla. Add the dry ingredients slowly, stir them in. She had no chocolate, but she didn't need any.

She got the sharpest knife from the rack and slit her wrist over the bowl.

Add one and a fourth cup of your own blood. Mix thoroughly.

She bandaged herself up and put the cake into the oven. Outside the neighbourhood was getting noisier and noisier as people gathered in the streets.

Let the cake bake for one minute of every year of your life.

Thirty minutes.

Her timer went off and she opened the oven and out poured black smoke that billowed around the kitchen, stuffing itself up Bonita's nose, making her cough. Then from inside the smoke crawled out a small blood-red creature. It had limbs like a cat and feet like a reptile. Its body was smooth and spongy. Two small horns adorned its head, and lashing behind it was a long and pointed tail.

Bonita spoke softly.

'Don't worry about being seen, and be careful to evade their traps. I want you to go and eat every single lemon on every single tree in this neighbourhood.'

The creature looked up at her, its eyes only small divots in its face. It bowed and then leapt away, crashing out the window and howling into the early night.

Bonita laughed and laughed and laughed. She clutched her bandaged wrist then after a few beats ran outside.

She could hear screaming in the distance and the sick wet garbling of something being swallowed.

The group at the front of Carl's house turned and shouted, and Carl took his gun from his back and brought it in front of him.

'What the hell is that?' he yelled.

The creature's body was now bulbous and lumpy and significantly larger than it had been before. The neighbours screamed and Carl aimed his rifle and took a shot at the beast.

A hole opened up in its abdomen and several lemons tumbled out, but it did not deter the creature in the slightest.

Bonita watched as it grabbed hold of a tree that still bore some fruit and ripped the entire thing out of the ground. It shoved it into its throat and then pulled it out bare.

She expected most of her neighbours to run, but at the next house the beast came to, before it could rip up the lemon tree, a woman ran out and threw herself in front of it.

'You will not!' she cried. 'Not my tree! Not mine!'

The creature considered her for a moment. It looked at the lemon tree, then back at her, and then with its great big claw it grabbed her, opened its wide mouth, and swallowed the woman whole.

Bonita could not believe her eyes. The rest of the people on her street screamed.

The creature paused and considered this new taste. It moved towards the rest of the crowd on the street.

'Stop!' Bonita cried. 'Stop it!' But the creature paid her no mind and continued advancing.

'Shoot it!!' Bonita called out to Carl who was stiff with shock. He flinched and fumbled with his gun to take another shot at the creature.

Another hole opened in its body and a few lemons tumbled out but nothing more. It reached out with its meaty paw towards Carl. Carl shot at it again but missed as he was snatched up and thrown into the beast's mouth.

Bonita watched the lump of Carl's body move through the creature's throat like a digesting snake.

Instead of running, everyone else near her went up to the front of their houses, their stance wide and hands spread in an attempt to protect their trees.

'What are you doing?' Bonita said. 'Run!!'

The creature picked up and swallowed yet another person, its abdomen swelling.

Bonita squeezed her eyes shut, mind whirling, then froze as she thought of something.

The creature's body was made of cake, and it only stopped eating lemons because it tasted something it liked better.

She ran towards it in a wide arc. It was so focused on the people in front of it that it didn't pay her any mind.

She reached its rear where she grabbed the end of its tail and began pulling on the end, feeling its spongy skin under her hands. The creature stopped its pursuit of her neighbours and turned its attention towards her. Then just as she predicted it brought its head over towards her and its tail; its mouth open and gaping, ready to swallow her whole. When it almost reached her she leapt to the side and released the end of the tail as it entered the creature's mouth.

It didn't seem to understand that this was part of its own body and bit it off with ease, swallowing the thing into its massive maw.

Bonita panted, her heart thumping in her ears. She watched the creature contemplate its next step. It stood there, computing, and then once again it raised its head, opened its wide jaws and stuck the end of its tail in its mouth.

The sound it made was horrible: crunching and garbling and wet with the smell of lemons permeating the air. It bit off another piece and another. When it reached its abdomen lemons began pouring out along with wet piles of cake, and then the bodies of the three neighbours it had eaten. It slowly was turning itself inside out.

At the end of it all, all that was left was a pile of cake and lemons and blood. It undulated once where its mouth had been, then fell still.

Bonita sank to her knees. Her hands trembled.

That was it, she thought. That was the end. She wasn't sure what it was the end of. She wasn't sure if anything had changed, if anything was ever going to change.

Then out from behind her, loud and clear a voice said: 'Bonita Anne Vertrees. Come here right this instant.'

It took a moment for her to compose herself, to register the words that were spoken. Then she obeyed. She was happy to. She stood up and turned around and walked towards the front door of her house where her mother stood with her hands on her hips and her face in a frown.

When Bonita reached the door her mother said, 'You are grounded, young woman. Get inside.'

Bonita went inside and she washed up and did the dishes. Her mother took Bonita's phone and said, 'No job searching, no internet.' The two sat in the living room while the TV was on, and Bonita cried and cried and cried. Her mother patted her head while she did.

Outside in the neighbourhood, the bodies that lay in the carnage of the beast sat up and walked to their respective homes feeling not quite like themselves. They showered and went to bed and did not speak of it, of anything.

The Readers

Jonathan Page

The snow blackens the hedges and the house and the green tin barn. It yellows the sheep and the strewn bales they feed on. It makes the ridge shine under the bluish platform of the clouds. It stings Tom's throat and burns his eyes and fingertips. It sits crushed in the folds of his coat and removes him from his feet in his double-socked boots. It makes the black dog blacker and all back and ears unless he jumps, swimming, through its depths. It is a job to get the hay out on such days. It is a job to check on the sheep who die so quietly in drifts and piles against the buried walls. It is a job to get the hot milk across the slipping yard into the house. It is a job to even keep the kitchen warm, where his mother sits swaddled in front of the range and seems to read the same page over and over of her illegal book. But then most books are. But then nobody cares to report them for such trivia, because why? They are alone up here. They do as they have always done, these past fifteen years. They survive, and put their faith in deep time, in sheep and cattle and the passing of all things.

Tom feels a pressure in his ears, which becomes a dark noise and a mobile shadow over the straggling white box of the field. He squints up, sees a shining black beak looking back at him. The drone is as long as the house, a dirty green, a man with spread arms. There are slender missiles and the striped eggs in its black claws and he smiles until his jaw hurts, as if the drone was a friend, or a colleague; and the noise throbs in his ears and the drone leans backwards at last, becomes a man stretching, and falls away into the valley.

He whistles to the shouting dog to bring her tunnelling close to his heel and covers her brow briefly with his half-gloved snow-raw fingers to reassure her. The sheep are gone over the brow of the hill and must be fetched back before they tumble into the drifts. He must fetch himself back to the sobriety of the task in hand. No damage has been done. No damage. A section of pristine snow has been tumbled away by the rotors, that is all. God, please still my hands.

*

His mother, Jan, has not moved: she is a shape over the open fire gate, her book – poetry again – wobbling in her hands. She is a blue eye under the blanket and wisps of transparent hair. Tom makes his acorn coffee and sits beside her in his hard elm chair. The dog weighs on his feet. He sips his drink and after a while pushes a log into the fire. Her coffee goes undrunk and he will drink it too if she does not.

His father, a smiling fat man in a black doctoral gown, is a framed photo over the kitchen table. He lifts his cup and mouths: *To you, Dad*. Soon enough he will see only snow-light in the flaked white bars of the windows. His dog will transform into a black rug and his mother's book will glow in the half-light. His mind will turn to the farm again: to the basics, to food and fuel and the health of their small flock, the six milch cows in the shitty warmth of their barn.

What did the drone want? Nothing.

To look at him.

To make him afraid.

Afterwards, Tom goes from room to room throwing books into holdalls. He sweeps the small bookshelf in the chill unlived-in living room with the back of his hand and lies on his side to probe the spaces under the cupboard and sofa for dropped and foot-nudged books. Poets mostly. Novelists who write about divorce and love affairs in a world long gone. Lethal marginalia. Ludicrous death sentence stuff.

He goes in his socks up the narrow stairs to his stark room, the divan held in place by tractor weights to stop its slow migration over the bowed floor. He bags his own books more carefully, out of love. There are pictures on the walls, safe ones, nothing abstract or too fancy-good. Nothing to make a visitor think too hard or suspect a latent wokeness. Still, he inspects each faded image in turn, palming off the dust and the cobwebs clinging to their backs and frames.

When he has filled three bags with books he carries them out to the shed where everything broken or redundant is dumped. The day burns red in the trees over the brook and the shining field. He pushes the bags under the feedbags and moves the long-dead quad bike across the doorless inner door as if that should deter.

Tomorrow or the day after or the day after that when the sameness of their days, his routine, reasserts, he may retrieve them again. Because really, where is the danger in books? After all these years.

His mother stirs the burnt-lipped pot. She wears her blanket like a cloak and her scarf still hides her face, but she is upright at least, making supper. She understands his mood, though he has only spoken of sheep and the broken wall he will mend on the thaw. He collected the books while she slept, all except the splayed poetry – John Berryman, Henry and Old Bones soothsaying the world to come – she had in her hand. But this too he takes, hiding it behind the plastic-wrapped pallets of cans in the pantry.

This is their mantra: there is no tech in the house, no radio even, because tech listens to you and watches your fingers on the keyboard and the screen and wonders why you have purchased this item and not this item or thumbs-upped a picture of a near extinct animal or an influencer who has fallen out of favour. Because tech is why his father looks back at him from a photo and is probably long dead.

Tom sits opposite Jan at the square table, clunking his spoon through the stew, while the light dies beautifully, pink and orange, in the window. They are lit by oil lamps.

There are solar panels but they are old and weak and he does not know how to fix them or the battery they feed and they no longer have the money for experts. They turn on the electric lights only when necessary, for neighbours, say, who hardly come.

'Calm yourself, Tom.'

His mother glances at him over her bowl of stew. She looks at her spoon as if it puzzles her and sets it down again, clink.

'I am calm.'

'There have been planes before.'

'Drones, Mum.'

'Drones then.'

'None that looked me in the face. I smiled at it like an idiot.'

'So? That was the right thing to do. They'd come for sure if you hid your face.'

'They may come for us anyway.'

'Nonsense.'

'Like they came for Dad.'

'That was long ago. Long ago. And that was Dad. So long as we don't go anywhere, do anything other than live our lives, we're fine.'

His mum, skeletal, raw-skinned, blonde and white, scrapes back her chair and, feeding the table through her long hands, arrives by his side. She kisses the top of his head, where the hair thins, while he rakes the last of his three-day stew into a loose collapsing ridge. His mum strokes back his hair, makes him lift his chin; if she keeps going he may weep. She is right, he is being irrational. He does not know why he is afraid. It is just a feeling he has. It is the tiring snow and the blue-black freezing house. It is the discipline of endlessly repeated days and the living of a life not lived. But that thing stared at him for a long time, or so he felt.

*

From her black room, Ffion sees the black net over the white fields and the blink of streams, and then she is over the ridge, looking down at the delicately shadowed slopes and combes, at nothing, at blue-black swatches of trees and the blank grey eye of the reservoir. She dips to scatter a piss-yellow flock into a panicked vee then circles a grey farmhouse and its rusting green barn because she wants to. There are few delivery drones to monitor today, few trucks on the road, no reports of unlicensed movement. It is a quiet day, and there is only the joy of flying, of rolling quietly over the blank unchanging country. *Watch out* said her CO; the snow can fool you, there have been crashes before. But she is a good pilot, experienced, and she could do this in her sleep.

The man wades out on the broken tether of his path and his dog is a repeated puff of snow swimming alongside. The sheep stand stock then run again as she tips the delicate head of the drone to look more closely at the farmer. It is something to do. There is a quota and she is ten stars off a food coupon. How pathetic the man is: aging, raw-faced, feigning pleasure, as if she were an old friend or a wonder. He lifts a gloved hand and her thumb hovers, automatic, tempted, over the non-lethal array, but it is only a greeting of course. She yawns: the screen to her left is a blur of possible matches, a spinning green circle. All the politicos in the world seeking the farmer's face.

'Stop smiling, you dick.'

She sniffs and leans back in her office chair. The drone leans back as she does: her arms and the stiff cross of the drone synchronise briefly, accidentally. Then she drops the drone into the valley, slowly, gracefully, twisting it into the void.

'No sleeping for you tonight.'

The farm is already far away; there are a dozen little towns to buzz, a main road, and then she can turn for home. Her shift will be over in an hour. The system whispers in a soft American voice: *Thomas Costello, 47, single, agriculture sector, no speech, text or meme violations for 10+ years.* The man is clean. She opens her mouth to authorise an advanced search – it is a slow day and that fuck-me smile – but she is skimming the slumped and broken roofs of a village now and feels tired suddenly and wants to keep things simple. Tomorrow, maybe, on her non-fly day. A minor pleasure. Nobody is that clean, unless the man was a hermit. One of the amnestied? They couldn't deport all of them, could they? But her grasp on history is hazy. They do not teach history at the Academy.

*

The canteen is two storeys up in the old Senedd building and smells of old oil, coffee substitute and disinfectant. The runway is visible through the stained window, a neat grey bar in the centre of Cardiff Bay. AI will already have guided her drone to the hanger, but she sees two others, a small grey one, an urban spy, and a larger transport, lifting off into the greyness, as she carries her tray to the table. Drones are beautiful, modern and pure like few things in this world.

'How was it, budd?'

'Okay. Slow today.'

'The snow?'

'The snow. Keeps everyone indoors, doesn't it?'

'You take care now.'

'You too, sir.'

The CO is unreadably, smilingly pleasant at all times. She never really knows if she has said the right thing or the wrong thing to him. Some days he feels like a friend; but she fears him for his blandness. Colleagues have vanished without a word under his command, though she has no idea if he is responsible. He is slim, neat, quietly spoken, an aging mustard-haired man in an unmarked green jumpsuit, just like hers. She tries not to stare at his real coffee, the real bacon and eggs on his tray.

Her table is by the window, where she can watch the drones. She undoes her watch and lets it curl up on the table. The device is muted, though she can see the black-suited man as she eats, a man she does not know, walking the stage as they all do, smiling, passionate. *A New Way* says the curved blue-white screen at his back. *Together* says a second. *Prosperity* says a third.

The app is optional and at the same time mandatory: watching the leadership speeches is key to promotion; not watching means censure. So she cheats, like everyone else does, and leaves the watch playing silently to itself for hours at a time. Though it may not be cheating: the point of the app may be to force employees to adapt.

She spoons up the last of her reconstituted eggs and

wonders again about the smiling farmer. Too clean, too clean… She would love to please the boss if she can. To do something big and push way beyond food coupons. Sleet falls slow and slant into the slow grey water and the lights on the rust red wall that separates the city's slums from the three slim silver towers of the execs. One day she will live in one of the squat, brown officers' blocks, set hard against the razor wire fencing by the docks. The officers live a life without hunger or want and seemingly without fear. She would like, very much, to live like that.

Her CO carries his tray back to the rack and winks at her as he passes. She smiles back, a little too broadly.

*

The trees drip fat water onto the rain-carved road and rills run to either side of it, straightening the winter-sick yellow grass into lines under the water's dip and curve. A better day then, a brighter day; the sky a pale blue, the clouds pure over the ridge. The fields burn white and he squints at his boots as he drags his homemade sledge of fast-shedding hay. He whistles at the dog commuting hedge to hedge behind the ragged sheep, who come anyway, knowing him, seeing the hay. The sheep see-saw forward and pause and see-saw forward again.

It is a day like other days; he lives in his chores, in their expectation and commission, and rediscovers his balance. The fear brushes his heart still, his snow-hurt fingers. It makes him walk with greater delicacy, like an old man afraid of losing his footing. He slips on the stiff slick of mud breaking the ice in the trough and nearly does fall. But the fear is losing its hold, like the snow is losing its hold. His mother is right: where is the threat in them? Old lefties exiled to the hills. The world has moved on. He hardly knows what the world looks like now, beyond their valley, and has trained himself against curiosity.

After black tea and burnt toast, he goes out to the shed, over the water-shone yard, the deltas of tiny mingling streams. The stone house stands precise against the sky and the white mountains and he feels joy briefly. In another life he would write a poem to it. In his head he writes a poem. He judders away the half-hinged door and pushes the snub nose of the bike back into the stiff dark. It has been years since he picked up a protest book. They look new, lying there shinily in the gape of zip; he half lifts one up, *Live Free*, and another, *The Quiet Protester*, then lets them slip back over the pile like caught fish.

The online world fell so easily back then, was so easily compelled to censor and report, even the mildest forms of protest, jokes, memes about censored memes. Money allowed it. Money encouraged it, wanted it even. But for a while, in those last years, there was a surprise boom in book sales. Little presses springing up whack-a-mole style as the bans rained down. Banned books parties in living rooms and rented offices. He remembers the parties, the excitement, as if a few beers and earnest readings were the beginning of something unstoppable. There was an almost erotic quality to oppression because they believed against all evidence that it could not go on. That the country would simply turn against what it had voted for in such numbers. But change like that happened only in books, or in movies.

The Quiet Protester was Rebecca's book. *Live Free* was his. He cannot remember reading either of them, though he must have done.

Then Rebecca is there, standing stock in the charcoal shadow of their Cardiff flat, the street light orange in the glass-panelled door. He sees her long-sleeved jumper, her fine gold hair, the tilt of her head. He wondered later if she had known she would vanish: but she had shrugged, and smiled, and blamed a long day at the office.

She may have been deported – *Support migrants? Go with them*, said the apps – or disappeared into one of the new private prisons. She may have taken the bus to Scotland. She may have stopped loving him and not told him.

No. Not that. He cannot believe that.

Tom changes his mind, takes only a handful of novels and poets, and drags the bike back into place. He throws the empty feedbags back over the holdalls and a full bag of dog kibble for good measure. Later then, when the snow melts.

*

'How about pasta tonight, Tom? For a change.'

'We've enough?'

'We do. Spaghetti. Three packs at the back of the pantry.'

'You've been hiding it, Mum.'

'I have.'

Tom talks to his mother through a shut door. He is in the bath, the lukewarm solar-heated water topped up with kettles from the stove. His hands are bright red, his feet. There are unkillable cacti on the shelves at the far end of the room; a long inheritance, his mother's plants, transported from house to house to house when so much else was abandoned and lost or sold. There is poetry, the old dream, the former dream, that does not know it has died, stacked on the stool next to the bath.

Steam in his glasses so he cannot read for long without wiping them clean and steam in a fat mobile tower over the length of the bath, boasting comfort, heat, though if he lingers longer the cold on exiting will be torture.

The image of Rebecca comes again, her head tilted, the jumper that half covered her hands, though less forcefully; a gentle image, uninterrogated. She stands over the pages of the book and prevents his taking in of the difficult words and he sighs, darkly, loudly, surprising himself, when he thought there was no feeling.

She is gone.

She is gone.

She is gone.

And there is no retrieving. It is no good; tomorrow, or the next day, he will think of her again and believe that she is out there somewhere, searching for him, or waiting to be found.

'Tom.'

'What?'

'I thought I saw something.'

'What?'

Silence. He listens to her bump and shuffle, the clatter of pans, coming up through the bathroom floor. He goes back to his book: one more poem and he will get out of the bath.

'Tom.'

He pulls a towel around his waist and thumps downstairs to the kitchen. His mother is staring out the window, a tea towel fisted into a pan. She turns to him, and smiles, faintly.

'What's up? What do you see?'

He sees the looping wire of the washing line and the bird table heaped high with snow and the logs stacked neat and various in their pallet-built shelter. Only sky, only a hurl of black birds and the slushy ground.

'There was a grey whirry shape over by the trees. I thought it was a drone.'

'A little one.'

'Like the old delivery drones, you know. Small.'

157

'It could be the tree, the wind, you know.'

Silence.

'My eyes aren't good at a distance.'

'Yes.'

Still, they continue to stare. But the chill is sharp in his chest and there is only the quiet day and the snow and the kitchen smells. He touches his mother's arm and pads back upstairs to dress.

*

Ffion sips real coffee in her faded baize enclosure in the low wide brown office. The CO brought it to her himself. He set it down next to her workstation and said nothing, only touched her shoulder. The coffee is extraordinary, richer tasting than she remembers, more bitter. But it is the favour of it that makes her blush, his coming and going from the crowded office to mark her out to the others.

The farmer is still a nobody, even after all her digging, but the mother. The mother. She is Doctor Margo Costello, 74, former Senedd, former Green, former media star. She organised god knows how many protests back in the day and went to prison for a decade. One more infringement, however slight, means life. To take her down would be a coup; she had been forgotten but now she is found.

'Show me the raid map.'

The AI blends video from the elderly local police drone into a sweeping movie of the house and barn. It flags doorways with helpful green lines and adds a hedgehog of red lines to windows. It recommends a path up the lane and across the yard.

'Show me faces.'

And there they are, the farmer in a towel, the old woman

with a pan for a hand. She is surprised by a momentary pity – she thinks of her own mother beyond the wall – then remembers the coffee she cradles in her hands.

*

Tiny balls of snow tumble away from the soldiers, plunging and swaying up the hill. The snow carries long images of the green and pink trees and burns orange at the curve of the hill. It is harder going than they imagined: their leader throws a tiny drone, no larger than a butterfly, to learn what they already know, that there are stone walls and more snow to come. The sun is a white ball breaking on the ridge and it is night still in the woods and valley. Their noses sting with cold.

Ffion is in the butterfly, and in all the butterflies the soldiers and police will use today; anything larger might alert the Costellos, though where would they go? To have them stumble out into the snow would make for a good media post later. But this is raid protocol, and she has been taught all her life never to question rules.

She switches views and switches views, going from one straggle of figures to another and then back again, sees walls, and more walls, and whiteness, and wet black gulleys jammed with stones and bones. She expects the farmer at any moment, to see him make an 'o' of his lips and reach out to the creature that contains her, as he did in her dreams last night. He does not appear. He will not appear. It is dawn and the drifts are still deep, and even if he is up, he will surely stick close to the house and his flock.

The house and its green barn appears, neat and angular in the dip. The stream that runs black and silver at the foot of the yard. Switch, switch, switch; the teams are nearly in position and the house remains blind to them. There are no lights in the windows. Anything may condemn the old woman; a hard drive, a diary, the wokeness of a book.

'Stand by, Blue.'

'Stand by, Green.'

She turns the butterflies to survey her troops, ski-masked, helmeted, kneeling as they unhitch and sight their weapons. She jumps into their helmet cams to join them – the CO, monitoring the op from his office, will see what she sees – when they run rattling and screaming into the yard and kick open the farmhouse door. One minute to go. Thirty seconds.

'Wait, what is that?'

The slats of the slumped shed are suddenly scarlet, and grey smoke leaks from the whitewashed stones and rusted tin roof. The farmer walks calmly into view, a long black coat carrying a metal pail; he leaves the yard as if he did not see them crouching there among the stubby trees and lays the pail in the stream and picks it up again. The soldiers run towards him; one slips onto his back on the sodden slope. There is time for Tom to hurl a symbolic pail at the foot of the shed before they are upon him.

*

'You started that fire. I can smell the petrol.'

'You saw me try to put it out. There was valuable stuff in there.'

'Like what?'

'My spare solar battery was in there. My quad bike. Petrol cans.'

'Don't get clever with me.'

'I'm not being clever.'

Tom and his mother sit at the kitchen table, their wrists

bound with plastic ties, while the raiders pull down cupboards and throw kitchen drawers to the floor.

'We are good citizens.'

He looks at the soldier's helmet cam and smiles and Ffion feels herself blush. She jumps into the farmer's bedroom where a police officer tears a long cross in the mattress with her knife. She jumps to the back of the kitchen where a soldier pulls an iron casserole down on himself.

'We'll see about that.'

The hours pass. No papers of any kind, bar a few feed bills, are found. No computers, no books. No watches or old phones in bottom drawers. The soldiers go out into the barns and outbuildings and walk the water-destroyed lanes and kick through the cracking orange deltas of the vanished shed. The old woman asks to go to the toilet and is refused and her urine pools on the red tiled floor. The farmer is punched in the ear and then kicked off his chair but says nothing. The soldier who punched and kicked him helps him back up and cuts the ties on his hands, then the ties on his mother's hands, and pats them both on the back.

Ffion jumps from camera to camera to camera to camera to camera. She is still jumping when the CO messages her to come through to his office.

A week passes. Tom and Margo wait for a follow-up raid, for revenge. Their conversations are stilted, whispered, always on mundane subjects, in case the house is bugged. They write notes to each other on the backs of feed bills. They search under lampshades and furniture and pull up broken boards and find nothing. Apps are the thing, phones, and the authorities can sit a mile away and listen to them anyway with the tech they have. They go back to talking as they always have.

The snow has melted away to strips and curls under the

walls and hedges. Tom scans the paling blue sky and walks under a dissolving ball of hay towards the rusted feeder. The sheep flow down out of the relative shelter of the trees; their tough lips pull the hay from his hands even as he lofts it into the cage. He keeps his arm buried in the hay until he finds the holdall and pulls it free and brings it to his chest so that the flaps of his open coat part-shield it from view.

There was no sleeping, try as he might, that night before the raid. He had risen at midnight and laboured out into the dimly glowing fields, under the cold-fuzzed stars, to stash bags – this was Margo's idea – in the hay feeders. One bag, the next to last, he had buried deep in the warm, gently smoking midden, because he was wet from falling and wading and very cold. The unborn day was a grey band across the hilltops by then and he no longer believed anything would happen. Then it did. He looked back, yawning, at the trees and saw a single hovering blue pin of light. The last few books, the political ones, the most dangerous, were still in the shed, but he had soaked the place in petrol as a precaution and the fire caught quickly.

'What have you got there?'

Margo, smiling, pulls books from the bag as soon as he sets it on the table. It has been so boring for her, with nothing to read. Her blanket falls to the floor.

'Novels, mostly. Mantel, Enright…'

'All right. I can see for myself, Tom.'

It is like Christmas; he finds a bottle of wine in the potato cellar and fills two water glasses. They pile up the books on the table in full view of the window and choose a book each to read by the stove – a Duras for her, an Erpenbeck for him. His fear is gone and so, he thinks, has hers: there is no reason to believe that they are safe, and every reason to think otherwise. But they are, he feels it. There will be no more drones this year.

Activity Week

Sybilla Harvey

The coach from Cymla to Craig y Ddinas took an hour longer than expected. One of the boys vomited into an old ashtray attached to the back of a teacher's seat. It overflowed and made its way down the steps and towards the door. They pulled over. The driver popped the windows, including the roof vents, and the coach exhaled as the engine was switched off, a great whale surfacing above the blue.

When the centre confirmed no one would come for the unwell boy, the driver called in a favour from a smaller coach to take him back. As it drove away, the other boys did not wave, only the accompanying teacher, glad to be returning. Instead, the boys made several hand gestures at the smaller coach, talking amongst themselves about why it was called flipping the bird, while the remaining teacher did her best to wipe up. She used one hand to avoid getting anything on her new engagement ring, which appeared last week like a meteor in their lives. They all agreed it was a tragedy.

The driver walked up and down the aisle spraying a whole can of air freshener that smelled like everyone's nan. He had a way of breathing through his nose that was both bullish and vulnerable; he did not look like a healthy man: white shirt forced around his stomach and yellowed at the pits. One of the boys recognised that redness in his face, the clusters of blood vessels across his cheeks, and saw his own father asleep in hospital this last year. He looked away.

'Seats, please,' the teacher called, voice powerful and at odds with her slight frame. They called her the pixie and often talked about her cropped, white-blonde hair.

The coach door hissed closed and one of the boys sang the music from *2001: A Space Odyssey*. It played at the centre last month but had to be stopped because the boy with the laser pointer kept shining it at Gary Lockwood's face. The coach pulled out of the lay-by and back onto the road. Some said what sort of prick does that in an ashtray. Another said who needs rivers and waterfalls when you had cascades of puke. Then they laughed at the boy who said cascade and called him a prick too.

*

The driver left them standing in a car park, rucksacks on, waterproof zips grazing stubble and dreams of beards. A large sign welcomed them to Waterfall Country. 'Wankers Ahead' was sprayed across it in red paint so a few got a selfie. Then phones were collected and dropped into the centre's travelling lockbox. Grey and heavy, it was the kind of light that made no one look good: the boys had a pallid sheen; even the teacher appeared sallow, despite a week in Greece and the glow of impending marriage. They stood awkwardly, arms wrapped around themselves. One chewed the side of his fingernail while another refused to take off his headphones. Heads were shaved close; hair was artfully sculpted into spikes; one boy had managed to grow his. It fell in a lank hazel ponytail which some of the boys called Cindy.

The teacher did a headcount, ten in all. A copse of boredom, hormones, and tracksuits. A few felt the dank chill run down their necks; others wished they hadn't eaten their lunch before they even made it across the Gnoll. Most stared at the towering cliff at the end of the car park, isolated and ancient. They'd seen pictures of it back at the centre but never appreciated its majesty, its fuck-off size. A few said there's no way they were climbing that, and they'd sooner walk back to Cymla.

A man in a van flashed his lights and the boys turned to each other and knowingly whispered: dogger.

'Ignore him, Miss,' one said. 'Wants a shag.'

She relaxed at the sight of the glowing head beam. It was rare there was just one teacher with a group of ten boys. While it was still legal, it was not recommended.

'That must be Byron,' she said, waving.

A man climbed out of the van, a figure as tall and taut as a guide rope. He wore an expensive-looking fleece and waterproof trousers, which the boys had all been asked to bring but chose to forget.

'Here they are!' he said, raising a hand, voice ravine deep. 'I was worried I'd got the wrong day.'

The teacher shook his hand and apologised for the delay, explaining. She hoped they could make up the lost time.

'No bother at all,' he said, sizing up the boys. They stared back.

There was a round of intros. Even the most confident were surprised at how nervous they felt when it came to saying their name aloud and whether they'd done much walking or climbing in the past. The boys who had been bouldering a couple of times in Swansea told Byron they were probably intermediate level and not beginners, and Byron said fantastic, you'll be teaching us then. The teacher laughed and said I hope not.

He ushered the boys over to the boot of the van and revealed a trove of ropes, hard hats and clips. There were bags of chalk, harnesses and a blue crate of spare shoes. It felt like a problem they had to solve.

'Now, son,' Byron said, gesturing to a boy at the back of the group. 'Would you be up for switching those?' Byron pointed to the boy's black shining shoes, soles smooth and new. 'I'd be worried about you slipping, is all.'

The boy couldn't find his trainers that morning so he wore the ones he had for his aunt's funeral a few weeks back. The boy said yes, he would ta, and when Byron said what size, reaching for the blue crate, a few of the boys laughed and shouted the smallest you've got By, and the boy said I'm a size 10 actually.

'Changing rooms and lockers are over there,' he said, gesturing to a breeze-block building behind them. The teacher said they wouldn't need to change; they came ready to climb, but could she leave the lockbox in the van, and the boy's shoes?

A few listened to Byron's run-through but not many. They were keen to walk, not only because they were cold and spring still felt like winter, but because instructions like this didn't sit well with anyone on the trip. The teacher thanked Byron and hard hats were distributed. They were the same yellow as the MDMA in one of the boys' rucksacks, stolen from an older brother's jacket. It was agreed they'd make their way to the crag.

'The main face is great for first timers,' Byron said.

Those who were still virgins, which was most, felt targeted with the reference and their cheeks rushed with heat. Souls shrunk like crisp packets in an oven. The boys looked to the ground, and kicked at the glint of a Wrigley's wrapper, the plastic rings of a six pack. The teacher said get a move on.

They neared the towering slab of rock, the size of at least two big houses around St David's Park. It was limestone according to the teacher, but to them it looked like the end of the road, something impenetrable and not worth messing with.

'Right then,' Byron said.

One of the boys had the urge to leap over the fence separating the slab from the car park, to kick it and snap the wood like a twig. He did his breathing and forced the thoughts down into his body, which felt like getting toothpaste back into the tube. Byron looked at the slab like it was his first born and started talking about the anchors above and how everything was set up for them. The group squinted, a few noticing the winks of metal dotted around the crag. In the long snakes of ivy hanging over the stone, they noticed the other ropes, ready and waiting.

'We're nine,' the teacher said abruptly, spinning around. 'Why are we nine?' She did the headcount again.

'He's gone for a smoke, Miss,' they said and gestured to the boy leaning against the changing centre's breeze-block, rucksack at his feet. The teacher shouted for him to return.

'I don't care about the fags, just get back.'

'In a minute,' he called.

The boy let the nicotine zigzag in his blood, loosen his thoughts, and just as the teacher started walking towards him, he walked calmly towards her. The teacher picked and planned her battles with Napoleonic precision so said nothing once he returned and focused on the boys who had followed Byron under the fence.

The bouldering wall back in Swansea was pockmarked with red grips and welts. The boy whose father was in hospital felt like the joke was on him and he did not enjoy the experience. It seemed like the universe had dragged him there to draw attention to his own acne and hideousness. His mother had said no one is looking at you, everyone is concerned with their own problems, which he knew was a lie. But lined up in front of the smooth, dull silver of the stone and away from the indoor bouldering wall, the boy felt a peace seep through him. He ran a hand over it, cool to the touch and shining in places where people had gripped it before. He thought about the Iron Age hillfort the teacher said was at the top of the slab and imagined hands smaller than his (because everyone was smaller back then) touching this same stone.

'Who wants to go first?' Byron said and the boy felt himself say me.

They all laughed at the little harness. Byron kept saying this line would be bottom-managed by him. A few said steady on, By and they laughed some more, almost as hard as when Byron said buttress back in the car park. They were at the point in their lives where they were already tired of themselves. It was exhausting sifting every situation for something worth a laugh or dig. They knew they were taken on days out like this to focus, and for the most part they resisted it. Yet as they watched the boy size up the wall and grip it like a gecko, they fell into a welcome silence, plotting their own route upwards, seeking constellations in the stone which they could hold and make their own.

'Has anyone ever got to the top?' the boy with the borrowed shoes asked.

'Take your time,' Byron said. 'Think it through. You're locked in and safe. What's stopping you?'

The teacher took out an old digital camera marked with the centre's orange tape and began taking photos, the flash aggressive and annoying. Before he reached halfway, the boy with the thoughts like toothpaste said he was coming down, an unexpected jolt of vertigo pulsing through him. Byron steadied the line and took a few steps away from the slab, leaning backwards. The boy enjoyed the control he had over the line, the stop and start, that contradiction of being held in freefall. He landed lightly on the gravel and a few cheered. The boy looked to where he reached and was pleased with the effort. No one offered to go next. The teacher said they'd go in the order they were standing. She kept blowing into her hands because they were cold, turning her loose ring absentmindedly as she watched them. The air felt alive with their silence, their reaching and stretching for something to help them move forward. Like their handwriting, no one's climbing style was the same.

When she thought back to that day and the order they had climbed the rock, before they even got to the waterfalls, she still knew it like scripture. She can remember who reached where on the slab; who was angry with themselves for not getting further; which boys couldn't have cared less. The boy with the ponytail had slipped, overreaching, and dangled in the air with disappointment, refusing to move and suspended like a piñata. Byron stayed calm and said take your time, son, we've got all day, which the boy took to heart and delayed them by another forty minutes. The teacher's favourite, the one who wore his headphones everywhere, had only got as far as six or seven feet up before telling Byron he preferred to watch and was hungry.

The last boy to climb, the only one who made it to the top, was the boy who never said much or acted out. The teacher could never understand why he had been filtered into her class and out of the other school. Maybe he just hid it better than some. Whatever the boys had done, they had done it more than once. They were repeaters, mythmakers, but the boy, as far as she knew, didn't have a thing. Whether it was because he had time to plan his route or whether he just didn't stop to think and gave his all, the boy reached the top anchor in what felt like a minute. Byron said fucking hell then had to apologise to the group. It was impressive; the boy's body stayed so close to the stone, he clung like the ivy, his grip as rooted as the tree above. They all said he might as well have done it without ropes. Before descending, he dangled with one hand and waved to them, then slowly hopped down the wall to the inevitable cheers and prick-calling. The teacher remembers how he smiled to himself; the click he did with each knuckle when he was unclipped and surrounded by the boys; and how when Byron asked who taught you that because I'd like to shake their hand, the boy said: secret.

*

Byron led them uphill along a soft, mulchy path, canopied with green and leading to the waterfalls. There were multiple signs for picnic spots, but he said the best one around here was near the bridge as you could hear the water, and it was a nice way to eat. There was also usually less litter. A few of them wondered what a nice way to eat meant.

There were no benches but the ground was dry, so they sat in a circle. The centre had a big round table they often ate around, grooved with writing and the time the boy with the headphones stabbed a knife into the wood. Those who had eaten theirs on the coach had a couple of the spare sandwiches the teacher packed last minute. They downed cartons of apple and pulled water bottles from their rucksacks.

'Stop chewing so loud,' one said.

The boy with the laser pointer told them all the ham in these sandwiches came from his dad's abattoir, which they said was disgusting. The day had brightened and along with the faint smell of sweat, the group had acquired a pleasant tiredness, like an edge had been chipped off.

'Can I have my phone, Miss?' one asked. 'I need to make an emergency call.'

'No, you don't,' she said.

'You do this every day?' the boy with the MDMA asked Byron, offering him some of his crisps.

'Rain or shine,' Byron said, taking one. 'It's just a hike if it's wet though. We have another group early tomorrow morning, then one straight after. Unusual it's just you lot to be honest but Mondays are quieter.'

The boy who went off to smoke took out a lighter from his rucksack and began flicking the wheel until it sparked. The teacher stopped talking to the boy beside her and silently reached out her hand. The flame looked pale in the daylight and tremored with the gentle breeze. Everyone was silent.

'You'll have it back later,' she said but he held up the lighter like a torch. The teacher didn't speak, just kept her arm straight. The diamond of her ring caught the light, sparking its own rainbow. It fell across the boy sitting opposite her. 'Drop,' she said.

The boy didn't drop the lighter and they all watched the colourful ray. The boy with the laser pointer could not look away. He felt the same way about the boy with the rainbow on his face as he did about Gary Lockwood in *2001: A Space Odyssey*. He wanted to keep looking at him forever.

'What you looking at?' the boy with the rainbow said, already self-conscious after saying cascade. 'Cut it out.'

'Lighter please,' said the teacher.

'He's the one with it, Miss, not me,' the boy with the rainbow shouted.

'I know that. Hand me the lighter now or we don't move onto the next part.'

The boy tossed the lighter to the boy next to him. It was

slowly ferried around the group until it made its way to the teacher who put it in her rucksack. Still self-conscious, the boy with the rainbow focused on the thin gold chain around his neck, a 15th birthday present from a girlfriend. He grabbed it with his mouth, and it stayed there like a horse's bit.

The group were quiet for what felt like too long, until Byron produced a map of the area and showed them where they'd be going next. The teacher asked about time and if they'd do it in two hours and Byron said easy, no problem. A few of the boys said they were staying there and didn't fancy the walk. The teacher said in their dreams.

'You think this is my dream, Miss?' one asked.

The boy in the borrowed shoes had blisters, not from Byron's spares, but his funeral shoes. In the crematorium, he had felt guilty for thinking about his feet and how they were killing him, and not his aunt up there in her coffin, or his cousins crying in the front row.

'Can we just go climbing again?' the boy with the ponytail said and Byron let out a happy howl that made them all jump.

'Someone's caught the bug,' he said. 'We're walking now, mate, but you're always welcome back. Seven days a week.'

'How much is it?' the boy asked.

'I'll give you some info to take home.'

'No point, but ta though.'

Byron got everyone up on their feet and did a final sweep for rubbish, which felt like the only mountain he'd never conquer. Two hawks sailed above them, and above the birds a plane cut through the blue leaving a cloud trail behind it. The boy whose father was in hospital said his dad was convinced that those lines in the sky was the government controlling the weather. What the actual, they said, and the boy said, I know.

*

The word 'waterfall' was flaunted so many times that day, when they finally did see one, climbing down the stone steps to the gorge, they were underwhelmed. They expected to feel it in their chests, the roar winding them. They expected it to look like the screensaver on the centre's computer, all that water clear and pure. The pool below, tinged with emerald, reminded the boy with the headphones of the crème de menthe he'd drunk at New Year's. His stomach contracted with the memory.

'Magic it is,' Byron said, waiting for their reaction. The boys stayed quiet. He seemed disappointed and for the first time that day, his demeanour sharpened. There was a sigh then a whisper to himself.

'Can't please them,' he said and walked ahead. 'Follow me,' he called. The teacher tried to ask some questions about it.

Stacked over three ridges, the waterfall was at least the size of one of the houses on St David's Park, but it was no Niagara. The water tumbled over the ledges as they went one by one down the polished stone steps, deeper into the gorge. Hands gripped the rail, some stinging from the climb earlier.

'Bit of a scramble,' Byron called from the bottom.

The gorge was blanketed with a dark green moss. Trees sloped across like they were trying to keep it safe or hidden. The teacher took a picture.

'Better?' Byron said.

The waterfall was louder here and the rocks vibrated underfoot. The air had a sweetness to it, the cool spray freshening their faces. It was also cut with something else: a bosky hue that felt private and bodily, which made them uneasy. More grotto than gorge, it had a kind of rawness you

173

didn't get at the Gnoll or Margam Park. The longer they were there, the more they understood, which is to say the less they understood. They couldn't find a hole in it. A welcome kind of confusion.

'It's good,' one concluded. Then another asked where the river went.

'That takes you to the hardest climbing in Wales,' Byron said.

'Can we go?' the boy who reached the top called. He had stepped away from the group and was scaling a section of rocks.

'Careful, mate,' Byron said then looked to the teacher. She called him back and he returned without making a fuss. 'I'd love to show you, but we wouldn't be back in time.' He checked his watch and nodded. 'Tell you what,' he said, pleased he had their enthusiasm again, 'we'll see one more thing. Just over the footbridge.'

'Is it the mine?' the boy with the headphones said, and Byron winked.

*

The night before, the boy with the headphones had spent hours looking at Byron's website. Light violet shadows fell under his eyes from not enough sleep. The homepage had a serious climbing introduction from Byron. He said that technique and perseverance are needed, as much as power and guile. The boy had looked up the word guile, then after he got the measure of Byron, he clicked into a map of the area, dropping down into the gorge, clicking around until he reached the footbridge they all walked across, Byron up front, the teacher at the back. He clicked on and on until he reached the mine. Even on the satellite images there were 'Keep Out' signs everywhere. He clicked like a May-bug on a window trying to get the camera to go further. It stopped in front of the mine's entrance, a black and gaping mouth supported with steel.

Like the main slab, the entrance was sectioned off with a cowering fence, but the 'Keep Out' signs had fallen. They all ducked under, already feeling the change in temperature. The teacher shook her hands again to warm them. Byron adopted a sombre tone as he talked about people who once worked there, and they all agreed it was grim. As Byron explained about silica, the boy with the toothpaste thoughts pushed past the group and into the mine, over the stone slabs and onto a softer, chalkier floor.

'Careful, lad,' Byron said firmly. 'Best come back now, son.'

The boy felt like a valve inside him had been released, and the urge to keep doing something he shouldn't shimmered before him. He was barely ten metres in, but the rush flooded his body. The teacher called but he didn't hear; the hard hat had quietened everything.

'Get back here now,' the teacher shouted, louder this time, but the boy went further into the mine to the point where it split into two small tunnels, each of them leading to another black hole. The teacher stood at the entrance.

'It's not funny now, mate,' Byron called, but the boy was out of sight. He was laughing and crouching in one of the smaller tunnels, daring himself to go further. Byron took a torch from his rucksack.

A few boys called for him to get back. The teacher tentatively stepped over the threshold and shouted again. She clasped her hands around the back of her neck while she paced. Byron said something to her then walked into the mine, torch illuminating its scars. He walked slowly, calling to the boy who was now fifty metres or so into one of the tunnels, his breathing loud, hands holding the wet walls for balance. The torch disappeared into the black and the teacher kept calling.

The others stood at the entrance and the boy who reached the top felt pulled towards the dark. He moved swiftly to the right, ducking into the mine. A few boys noticed but didn't say anything to the teacher. Where the first boy had gone left, this one went right, holding out a hand to feel the calcified arc of the wall. Two more tunnels opened before him, a new level of darkness. Water dripped on his hard hat. The chinstrap had been digging into him all day so he took it off and placed it against the wall. He would go just a bit further, just to see. He was comfortable in the dark; it's where he learned to climb, roof running along Neath Town Hall at night, on the slate of the indoor market. He can't remember when he first looked at a building and knew he could climb it; how to scale it in as few moves as possible; the kind of jump it took to launch between sleeping freight trains. It was in him the way this mine contained whatever it was people wanted.

'Why are we eight?' the teacher shouted. 'Why are we eight?'

The boy with the borrowed shoes told her the boy who reached the top went inside for a look. His feet were numb and the pain from the blisters had stopped. For the first time that day he wasn't thinking about his shoes, which meant he wasn't thinking about his aunt and the crematorium chimney. The teacher brought her hands behind her neck again, edging on despair, then quickly pivoted, dropping to the ground in the time it took for the boy with the lighter to enter the mine.

'My ring,' she groaned, 'it flew off. Did anyone see it?'

She got down on her hands and knees and a few of the others did as well, combing the ground. They peered into the overgrowth. A broken bottle glinted and for a moment they thought they had it. The boys soon tired of looking and watched the teacher, her waterproofs muddied at the knees. Each of them made a calculation, weighing up the chivalric urge to do something for her or something for themselves. The boy with the MDMA was glad he swallowed some back at the waterfall. A creeping glee quietly rippled across his body. He took off his hat, scalp tingling.

'I'm pretty sure it went over there, Miss,' the boy with the ponytail called. He pointed to a stump. 'I saw it.' The teacher, desperate, turned her back again and scrambled over and around the stump. When she returned, they were gone, seven hard hats dotted across the ground.

*

Rusted hooks dangled from the mine's ceiling so they walked carefully. No one talked. The teacher screamed at the entrance. A few stepped in puddles but not the boy in the borrowed shoes who felt invincible. The boy with the headphones retrieved them from his bag and returned them, bug-eyed and black, to their rightful place like a crown. The boy with the laser pointer followed the boy he was in love with. Those who chose the tunnel on the left heard Byron calling but couldn't see a torch. No one minded the dark; eyes settled and adjusted. More turned left instead of right, which was just as well as the tunnels on the other side were tighter, and they'd have to walk one behind the other. They called for the boy who reached the top but there was no answer.

The boy who reached the top didn't care. You will always be someone's embarrassment, his old teacher said, which he found strangely freeing. He lay down, closed his eyes, pictured himself contained within this hulk of land. He hoped none of them would come this way. Finally, he had the kind of quiet he experienced high above ground at night, when he was sitting on the roof of his house on Cymla Hill, the town lights below like a pool of spilled orange juice. Occasionally, a metallic-tasting droplet hit his face. There was no room in this part of the mine for anyone except him. He didn't know how far down he'd gone. Grit sprinkled his shoulders. Somewhere, someone stepped in a shallow pool and shouted. The echo danced above him. The boy who reached the top felt held by the ground, lying there, arms by his sides. It had been a good day. He would come when called, but no one was calling, voices shrunk and moved further away. If he was to hold this feeling in his palm, this quiet, it would sit there like a cool, golden coin. He would hold out his hand to give the world a glimpse and say look, here it is, this thing I've been looking for.

Author Biographies

Ralph Bolland is an actor, writer, poet and dramaturg, with thirty years' experience in performing arts: from small-scale touring and theatre-in-education to regional Rep and the West End; from TV and radio to over a decade of community arts engagement. He was runner-up in the inaugural BBC Wales / NTW Drama Prize (2013) and has been published in *Red Poets* magazine and written Radio Drama for BBC Scotland.

Based in Llandrindod Wells since 2007, Ralph is Artistic Director of Mid Powys Youth Theatre, working to sustain high-quality, professionally-led arts engagement for young people in remote rural communities.

Born in Swansea and still there, **Alan Bryant** lives with his lovely wife in Mumbles. He has won the UK National Association of Writers' Groups historical short story competition, placed twice in their comedy prize, and had short stories published in numerous anthologies, with one nominated for the Pushcart Prize. His work has also been read on BBC Radio Wales. Many of his stories are based on humanity's failings, with some bordering on the zany side. He has a BA in Literature and Creative Writing from the Open University and writes without expecting Hollywood to napalm a path to his door.

Miranda Davies is a writer and academic. She has written many hours of radio drama for Radio 4; two novels (*Miss*

Treadway & the Field of Stars and *A Little London Scandal*) and a travel memoir. She publishes under the names Miranda Davies and Miranda Emmerson. She comes from a mixture of backgrounds, being at once Welsh, English, French, Polish and Jewish. She grew up in London but has lived in Barry, Vale of Glamorgan, for the past eighteen years. She is currently researching narratives around women's boxing at the University of South Wales.

Jonathan Edwards lives in Crosskeys, south Wales. His prize-winning poetry collections, *My Family and Other Superheroes* and *Gen*, are published by Seren, and his short fiction has appeared in *New Welsh Review*.

Sybilla Harvey grew up in Abergavenny and later completed an MA in Creative & Life Writing at Goldsmiths, University of London. Now a creative director for a production company in New York, she returns home often. Her short stories have been published in *New Welsh Review* and *Mslexia* and recognised in competitions such as the Berlin Writing Prize. She was a runner-up in the 2025 Rheidol Prize for Prose with a Welsh Theme or Setting.

Swansea writer **Natalie Ann Holborow**'s *Little Universe* was shortlisted for Wales Book of the Year 2025. She is a winner of the Terry Hetherington Award and the Robin Reeves Prize and has been shortlisted for the Rheidol Welsh Writing Prize and Cursed Murphy Spoken Word Award among others. Her writing residencies with the British Council, Literature Wales and Kultivera have seen her writing and performing poetry in Wales, Ireland, Sweden and India. She is the author of two other poetry collections with Parthian: *And Suddenly You Find*

Yourself and *Small*. Her first non-fiction book, *Wild Running*, is out with Seren in 2025.

Sian Hughes is a writer and creative practitioner working in schools and community settings. Her debut short story collection *Pain Sluts* was shortlisted for Wales Book of the Year 2022, whilst previous stories have appeared in *Storgy*, *Fiction Pool*, *Fiction Desk* and *Scribble*. Three of her stories have been adapted for the screen and broadcast on BBC Wales and S4C, with a recent adaptation of her story 'Consumed' winning Best Short Film at the Reykjavik and London BELIFE Short Film Festivals. Sian is currently working on a second collection, *Doll Skin*, and lives in Cardiff with her family.

Kate Lockwood Jefford grew up in Cardiff, worked as an NHS psychiatrist in London, and completed an MA in Creative Writing at Birkbeck. Her short fiction was awarded the VS Pritchett Prize (2020), 1st prizes in Bath (2021) and Brick Lane Bookshop (2023) Short Story Awards, and features in many anthologies including *Take a Bite: The Rhys Davies Short Story Award Anthology* (Parthian, 2021), *Aesthetica* (2021, 2022), and *22 FICTIONS: New Writing from Desperate Literature & Brick Lane Bookshop* (Cheerio, 2025).

Kate divides her time between London, Cardiff and Brecon, and is working on a novel inspired by the sensory and biographical landscape of south Wales.

Keza O'Neill grew up in Aberystwyth, where a love of stories took hold early – shaped by the people, the place, and a culture that values a good tale. She studied French in Sheffield and spent a decade hopping between London, Paris, and San Francisco, working in tech (but not the technical bit). Somewhere between airport lounges, luggage carousels, and client calls across 40+ countries, she rediscovered storytelling.

Her fiction explores the tangled threads between people and place, circling the idea of home. 'Sunny Side' was shortlisted for the Rhys Davies Short Story Award 2024; 'Lucky Strike' won the Sansom Award and placed third in the Bristol Short Story Prize 2023. Her work has also been longlisted for Mslexia, Bath, the CWA Debut Dagger, and Lucy Cavendish prizes.

She lives in Bristol — because home is just across the bridge.

Jonathan Page lives and works in the Black Mountains, near Talgarth. Several of his short stories have been anthologised in recent years, and he was shortlisted for the Rhys Davies Prize in 2022. His novel, *Blue Woman*, the fictional life story of a Welsh painter, was published by Weatherglass Books in 2022.

Tess Powell is a writer and artist from California who moved to Swansea, Wales to complete her MA in Creative Writing and continue her study of the Welsh language. She is new to her prose-writing journey and until now has mostly worked in illustration. In October Tess has a bilingual English/Welsh comic being released with the international Shortbox Comic Fair 2025 under the pen name 'Fortune's Fool'. She is always finding inspiration from the people she meets and places around her and has a penchant for writing about women at their wits' end.

PARTHIAN

Fiction

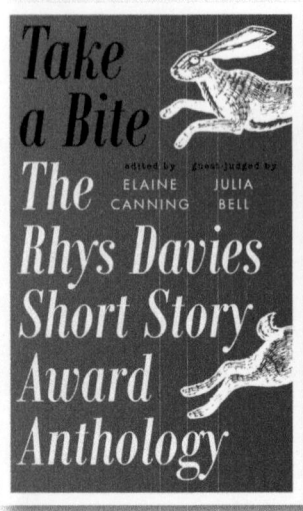

TAKE A BITE:
The Rhys Davies Short Story
Award Anthology

ISBN 978-1-913640-63-7
£9.99 • Paperback

THE TWELVE WINNERS OF THE
2021 RHYS DAVIES SHORT STORY
AWARD

CREE:
The Rhys Davies Short Story
Award Anthology

ISBN 978-1-914595-23-3
£10 • Paperback

THE TWELVE WINNERS OF THE
2022 RHYS DAVIES SHORT STORY
AWARD

PARTHIAN

Fiction

HARVEST:
The Rhys Davies Short Story
Award Anthology

ISBN 978-1-914595-74-5
£10 • Paperback

THE TWELVE WINNERS OF THE
2023 RHYS DAVIES SHORT STORY
AWARD

A DICTIONARY OF LIGHT:
The Rhys Davies Short Story
Award Anthology

ISBN 978-1-914595-83-7
£10 • Paperback

THE TWELVE WINNERS OF THE
2024 RHYS DAVIES SHORT STORY
AWARD

PARTHIAN Short Stories

Figurehead
CARLY HOLMES

ISBN 978-1-912681-77-8
£10.00 • Paperback

'Through beautiful, rhythmic prose
Figurehead weaves a sequence of stories
that are strange, captivating, and
unforgettable.' – Wales Arts Review

Men Alone
ÖZGÜR UYANIK

ISBN: 978-1-914595-82-0
£10.00 • Paperback

'This wry, moving, and beautifully crafted
collection of stories is a rich and
multilayered meditation on aloneness.'
– Tristan Hughes

Local Fires
JOSHUA JONES

ISBN 978-1-913640-59-0
£10.00 • Paperback

'Brilliant. A broken-voiced homage to the
towns we do our best to survive. Every
single story burns.' – Ben Pester

PARTHIAN Short Stories

Untethered
PHILIPPA HOLLOWAY

ISBN 978-1-914595-85-1
£10.00 • Paperback

**'A mood of ancient magic flits like
birds through these eerie and delicate
modern folk tales.'
– Samira Ahmed**

Take Three Canadians
GAIL HUGHES, TYLER KEEVIL,
TRISTAN HUGHES

ISBN 978-1-917140-76-8
£12.00 • Hardback

Four stories, three writers, and an artist

The Colonel Comes By
BRYONY RHEAM

ISBN 978-1-917140-80-5
£10.00 • Paperback

**'Skilled, perfectly formed, and compelling
... a deeply satisfying collection.'
– Karen Jennings**

PARTHIAN

RHYS DAVIES

RHYS DAVIES: SELECTED STORIES

Rhys Davies

"Gently wrapped, these stylish perceptive tales have centres as hard as steel, and are all the better for it."
– *William Trevor, The Guardian*

£8.99 / PB
978-1-912109-78-4

RHYS DAVIES: A WRITER'S LIFE

Meic Stephens

"This is a delightful book, which is itself a social history in its own right, and funny."
– The Spectator

£11.99 / PB
978-1-912109-96-8